CARNIVAL of the SPIDER

KIERAN LARWOOD

Illustrated by Sam Usher

faber

First published in 2023
by Faber & Faber Limited
The Bindery, 51 Hatton Garden
London, EC1N 8HN
faber.co.uk

Typeset in Times New Roman by MRules
Printed by CPI Group (UK) Ltd,
Croydon CR0 4YY

A CIP record for this book is available from the British Library

ISBN 978–0–571–36454–1

MIX
Paper | Supporting
responsible forestry
FSC® C171272

Printed and bound in the UK on FSC® certified paper in line with our continuing
commitment to ethical business practices, sustainability and the environment.
For further information see faber.co.uk/environmental-policy

2 4 6 8 10 9 7 5 3 1

KIERAN LARWOOD was born in Kenya. He moved to the UK when he was two and lived in various places before settling on the Isle of Wight, where he can still be found: exploring rockpools, climbing trees and writing. He taught Reception class in a primary school for fifteen years before becoming a full-time author. Kieran's books have won several awards, including the Blue Peter Best Story and the Prix Sorcières. He is inspired by a life-long love of fantasy stories, which all began when – as a young boy – he picked up a copy of *The Hobbit* and saw the map inside. It just goes to show – you never know where opening a book will lead ...

SAM USHER is a multi-award-winning illustrator. His books include the Seasons series, *The Birthday Duck*, *The Most-Loved Bear* and *The Umbrella Mouse*. Also a talented pianist, when he's not scribbling you'll find him perfecting a fiendishly difficult Chopin piece.

ALSO BY KIERAN LARWOOD

The Treekeepers

THE CARNIVAL SERIES
Carnival of the Lost
Carnival of the Hunted
Carnival of the Spider

THE WORLD OF PODKIN ONE-EAR SERIES
The Legend of Podkin One-Ear
The Gift of Dark Hollow
The Beasts of Grimheart

Uki and the Outcasts
Uki and the Swamp Spirit
Uki and the Ghostburrow

Podkin and the Singing Spear

Prologue

Even in the early hours of the morning, music can be heard. The echoes of laughter bounce down alleyways. The muffled tinkle of a piano, of glasses clinking, beautiful voices singing.

Paris is a city of painters, poets, sculptors, thinkers, writers, actors and playwrights. You can't throw a rock without hitting some kind of artist. And then they would probably write a sonnet about the sky falling on their heads.

But it is also a city of blood.

The pavements have run with it, are drenched in it. The walls are pockmarked by bullet holes, scarred by musket balls and sabres. There are splinters from barricades lodged in between the cobblestones. You can find the names of revolutionaries carved into the bricks.

Among all the glamour and wine and song, there is a steely edge. As if the Parisians are ready, at any minute, to leap for either a paintbrush or a rifle, and nobody knows quite which it will be.

It is a place of dazzling light and the deepest darkness.

As can be seen on this very night, in the Rue Chapon, a narrow street not far from the Gare du Nord, that colossal train station that links Paris with the world outside.

Shadows cover the cobbles, the shops and houses have their shutters closed and locked. But there, halfway down the street, a pair of tiny, pale hands emerge from an iron grille in the road.

They lift the metal grid, and a figure crawls out. Skinny, small – it is a child of no more than ten, dressed in torn and patched clothes, with a cap pulled low over his eyes. He stumbles to his feet, lowers the grille back into place, and then rests a moment, leaning against the wall.

Sobs are shaking his body. The muffled sound of his crying seeps down the alleyway, mixing with the far-off music. Making a sad song sound even sadder.

Then he stoops, presses a hand to the grille as if saying farewell, and staggers down the street. In his hand is a little round ball. A glint of white. Porcelain or china.

Once he has reached the end and turned into the Rue du Temple, the alley is silent, for a few heartbeats. Just the sound of several pocket watches quietly ticking.

You might think there is a watchmaker's in that road, that the noise comes from his stock, beating their little metal hearts behind a shop window.

But nobody sells watches in the Rue Chapon.

The noise comes from a group of figures, standing in the shadows at the far end.

They wait until the boy has gone, then one turns and speaks, a woman, her voice made hoarse and deadly with spite.

'You know what to do, Thom,' she says. 'After him. Now.'

The silhouette of a hulking man peels itself away from the edge of a building and begins to stalk down the street, trailing the boy like a bloodhound. A sound follows it – the soft clicking of clockwork parts, of springs and cogs, of oiled metal tapping.

  ... tickticktickticktickticktick ...

CHAPTER ONE

In which our new hero flees to London.

*F*ind her.

Those were the last words his mother had said to him.

Find Sheba.

He could still hear them, echoing behind him as he staggered forward, forcing himself to take one step after another, each one taking him further and further away.

Go to London. Find Sheba. Find the Carnival.

He had promised his mother he would do it. Promised he would leave her, even though he couldn't bear to. Even now, all he wanted to do was turn back, to climb down into that cellar again and curl up in her lap.

It didn't matter that she was chained and trapped, that he would be trapped with her. At least he wouldn't be on his own.

But you're not on your own. Not completely.

He looked down at the thing clutched in his hands. Once, long ago, it had been a porcelain doll. A Pierrot – a clown with a white face, black lips and a single tear painted on its cheek. It had been dressed in an outfit of smooth white silk, with gloved hands and booted feet. Now, only the head remained, and that had been cracked and glued and cracked again, until it was just a spiderweb of shards, the edges worn smooth by his worrying fingers.

Still, it was the only friend he had ever had.

'I'm sorry, Pamplemousse,' he whispered to it. 'I know I have you too.'

He reached the end of the Rue du Temple and looked both ways, wondering how he was going to get out of Paris.

This 'Carnival' his mother had told him to find – this 'Sheba'– they were in London. Somehow he had to travel across France and then the Channel beyond.

Him. On his own. The boy who had barely left his apartment.

'Shall I try and get a train, Pamplemousse?' It helped him to talk to the china head, even if it never replied. 'Or maybe I can find a cart going north?'

There was one, just up the road. A large wagon covered in canvas, being pulled by four horses. Some workmen had just finished loading the last of a stack of wine barrels, tying them all in place. It looked like the load was about to leave. At this time of the morning, it could only be heading out of the city, delivering its cargo to some distant place.

'There, Pamplemousse,' he whispered to the doll. 'That's my chance. Perhaps it's going to Calais? Then all I'll have to do is find a ship to England.'

The boy took a step towards it and then paused. He had heard a sound, not far behind him. A quiet ticking noise that was growing steadily louder. It could only mean one thing.

'They know I've escaped! They're after me!'

His soft steps turned into a sprint as he dashed across the street to the wagon. The last barrel had been tied in place, the workman was shutting the backboard and bolting it.

The boy ran up behind him, so close he would surely be spotted. But then, just as the workman turned at the sound of footsteps, the night seemed to shimmer and ripple. Inky clouds of shadow billowed from the sleeping doorways and windows, clotting together around the shape of the boy.

In a soft rustle, like bats' wings, he vanished from sight.

The workman shrugged, walking to the front of the wagon, just as the driver nudged the horses onward.

With a steady clop clop of hooves on cobbles, the wagon began to move, towards the main road out of Paris. And hidden among the barrels, still wrapped in his cloak of shadows, the boy peered out from the back.

He saw the figure of a man step into the road, standing on the very spot where he had paused just a second ago. *It's one of them*, the boy realised. One of his captors. *The one they call Thom*. Terrified, the boy held his breath, tried to will his heart still, as Thom's eyes looked up and down the street, searching for his quarry. And, as the man's head moved, the candlelight from a distant window caught and glinted on the side of his face. A metal face. A hinged jaw. A man who was more than part machine.

... *ticktickticktickticktick* ...

*

The wagon rolled on for several days.

Trundling along the dirt roads, the gentle rocking became like breathing to the boy, the space between the barrels his home.

Every now and then, they would stop at an inn or a stable. The drivers unloaded the odd barrel at a town here, a village there. But the boy and his china doll's head were safe in their darkness at the back.

He had heard the men talking, as the wagon plodded northward, and had discovered they *were* heading to Calais. Twenty-five of the barrels were bound for England, for London, just the place he wanted to go.

He was even able to reach under the canvas and occasionally pinch a few crusts of bread and a bite of sausage from their lunch basket. He felt terrible about stealing, but was worried that the noise of his rumbling stomach would give him away. Besides, he was sure they could spare a few crumbs and the odd swig of wine. Perhaps, when this was over, he would find them and give them a few coins to apologise. Perhaps.

Eventually, when the boy was beginning to think he might have to grow old among the barrels, they entered a busy city and pulled up at the docks.

From his hiding place, he could smell the salt of the sea, hear the *chuff chuff* of steam engines and the shouts of dockers and sailors. He could feel the sun, blasting out its last rays as it sank below the horizon. He could sense the cool lullaby of the night singing to him.

Darkness was his friend (unlike the burning, blistering sun). It soothed his skin and folded him into its inky shadows. He could hide away in it – soaking it up like a sponge until he became part of the gloom. Until the eyes of day-people slid off him, never knowing he was there.

That was his Gift, his mother always said.

Hers was being able to see without light and to move as fast as a striking cobra. She was brave and fierce and deadly – everything he wasn't – although it hadn't stopped the villains from catching her, and beating her and binding her with rope.

And she was still a prisoner: tied up in that mouldy, damp cellar with the rats. With those cruel half-people in the house above . . .

Oh, I hope they aren't hurting her. Just thinking of it made him want to turn round and run back to Paris, back to her arms. But *that* wouldn't help. Only completing his task would.

Go to London. Find the Carnival. Find Sheba.

Peering through a tear in the canvas, the boy watched the drivers walk into an office building, leaving the wagon unattended for a moment. Seizing his chance, he gathered the shadows close about him and slipped out of the back.

A stream of people were passing by: the day shift swapping places with the night. They were all too busy weaving in and out of each other, talking and laughing, to notice him as he crouched behind the wheels of the wagon.

'A ship,' he whispered to Pamplemousse. 'We need to find one going to England. To London, if we can.'

The doll looked up at him with the bright bead of his single eye. *Follow the wine*, he imagined it saying.

'Of course! The barrels are going to London. I just have to see which ship they're being loaded on to.'

Giving the doll's head a tiny kiss of thanks, the boy began to move, out from the wagon towards the stacks of crates and boxes waiting on the docks. He needed to find a space where he could hide and watch where they were taking the barrels.

... *tickticktickticktickticktick* ...

That sound again. Soft, hardly there. Blown across the docks on the hot wind and clouds of steam-engine smoke.

But the boy had heard it every wretched day of his captivity. It came from all of the monsters who had snatched him and his mother, who had bound them and kept them in that cellar. He would recognise it anywhere.

He scanned the crowds on the docks, looking for any signs of Thom. Of that half-metal face; the raw, puckered flesh where skin met steel.

There were dockers everywhere; all shapes and sizes, but none looked as though they had clockwork limbs or mechanical jaws. Had he imagined it? Would Thom have been able to follow him, all this way?

Maybe, maybe not. But he had to be careful, all the same.

Zigging and zagging, he dodged in among the mounds of boxes and barrels, hoping to throw any pursuers off the scent. He ran alongside a huge merchant steamer, one that was just being loaded. A large pallet of boxes was being lifted on a crane, about to be swung across to the ship's hold.

The boy didn't think twice. He leapt on to it, just catching the edge, and wormed his way underneath the tarpaulin that was holding everything down.

Up, up he swung, leaving the docks behind.

'We got away, Pamplemousse,' he said. 'But I have no idea where this ship is going. What if we end up in Spain? Or America?'

And that was when he noticed: the barrels he was crouching among were the same ones he had ridden alongside, all the way from Paris. Perhaps the moon was looking after him. Perhaps it was Pamplemousse. But, either way, he had chanced upon the right boat.

He was heading to London.

*

At least two days passed.

The boy could feel the chug of the steam engine, could hear the enormous paddle on the ship's side endlessly churning water. From where he crouched, hidden in the shadows between a stack of crates and the steel hull, his very bones shook as the lumbering machine ploughed through the waves, tearing its way through the water.

'Not much longer, Pamplemousse. I think we're nearly there.'

The tone of the engine had changed some time ago. The rhythm of the waves on the paddle wheel was slower, deeper. And then it stopped entirely until, with a groan and a shudder of protest, it began to turn in the opposite direction. They were reversing. Could they be sliding into dock? Was the journey finally over?

Chuff-chuff-chuff, went the boiler. *Clank-clank-clank*. Until, with a crash that clattered the roots of his teeth, the floating beast of steel and grease smashed against something solid.

'We're here,' he whispered to Pamplemousse. 'We made it. But now we need to get off the boat unseen.'

The shouts of the crew had begun, both inside

the ship and on the docks. Gangplanks were being lowered, hatches were hauled open, cranes swung this way and that, ready to unload the cargo.

Risking a peek around the pile of crates, he looked up to see a square of charcoal sky appear in the roof of the hold. Good. It was dark. Time to move. The boy didn't know what would happen to him if he was found, but it wouldn't be good. When day-people saw him, it never was.

'Every Gift comes with a curse,' his mother used to say, and *his* was the way he looked. That, and the screams that always followed whenever he was spotted.

The voices of the crew were louder now. They were coming down the steps, into the hold. Screwing his courage tight, he forced himself to slip out from beside the crates and clamber down among the cargo.

Don't see me. Don't see me. He began to repeat the words in his head, calling threads of darkness to wrap themselves around him. He could almost feel them: soft, cool tendrils, like floating wisps of seaweed. They flowed around his arms and legs, twisted across his body in plaits, drawing him into the deepest shadows.

When he felt as covered as could be, he held his breath, tucked Pamplemousse into his pocket, and began to make his way through the narrow pathways between the towers of wooden crates, teetering under their tarpaulins.

Up ahead were two crewmen, guiding down a crane hook from the hatch above. Crouching, hugging the edges of the cargo piles, he slid past them unseen. There was another man on the iron steps that led down from the deck above. He waited, hidden beneath the stairway, until the hulking sailor had stamped past in his hobnailed boots, before drifting up the stairs, quiet as smoke.

Stepping out on to the deck, he knew that the sun was just about to rise. The sky was lighter to the east but, more than that, he could *feel* it. An itch that began to creep over the bare surface of his face and hands. If he was still outside when the first beams of daylight touched him, there would be burns, then blisters as his skin cooked and flaked like hunks of meat on a grill.

'Oi! Nipper! Where'd you come from?'

Lost in his worries about the dawn, the boy had forgotten to hold on to the weaving. His cloak of darkness had fallen apart, leaving him exposed. And, of course, one of the crew had spotted him instantly. How could they not?

You idiot! he cursed himself, even as he started to run for the nearest gangplank. His mother would never have made such a stupid mistake. How was he supposed to rescue her if he couldn't even sneak around without being discovered?

Making himself as small as possible, he dodged past one sailor, then another. Hands like sides of meat swiped the air above his head, grabbing for his collar, but he was too quick – they missed him by inches.

'Stowaway!' someone shouted.

'Get him!' called another.

He crossed the deck in a mad panic, eyes wide with terror, his heart a hammering knot fluttering against his ribcage like a trapped bird.

Reaching one of the gangplanks, he started down, using the steep slope to give him momentum, to make his scampering feet even faster. At the foot of it was the dock and beyond that he could sense the cool darkness of more shadows. Scores of them, in between the brick warehouses and rickety cranes, underneath the carts and wagons that were being loaded and unloaded. They called to him, promising safety, offering to protect him from the eyes all around him and the cruel flames of the sun.

Just a bit further, he told himself. *If I can just make it a few feet more . . .*

He reached the end of the plank, leaping on to the brickwork of the dock – his first footsteps on British soil – and began to sprint towards the nearest alleyway . . .

. . . and that was when he stumbled. One foot tangled in the other, sending him sprawling, crashing into the legs of the broadest sailor in the whole of London. A second later, and the man's meaty fingers were snagged firmly in his collar, hoisting him up into the air as if he was a sack of cargo.

'Got 'im!' the sailor shouted, triumphant. Then: 'Nelson's eyepatch! Look at 'is ears! Look at 'is skin! What the 'eck are you supposed to be? Varney the Vampire?'[i]

But, before he could answer, the sun decided to rise. And the burning started.

*

Dangling in the air, being slowly choked by his own shirt collar, he could feel the dawn light begin to seep over his skin, bit by bit. It stung as it crept: it felt like his hands and face were being dunked in a bath of hot vinegar. Weak as the first rays were, he knew they would get stronger very quickly. He *had* to get out of the sunlight before that happened.

But there was no escape. Kick and flail as he might, the sailor had him in a lock-tight grip, holding him up for everyone to see. To his horror, a crowd was beginning to form. One that was being treated to a free early-morning sideshow.

'Look at it!' someone shouted. 'It's got ears like a goblin!'

'What about its eyes? They're red as rubies!'

'And its teef! Bless my muvver's bloomers, they're sharp enough to draw blood!'

'I told you already!' the sailor that held him bellowed. 'It's a vampire! They come through your window at night and suck your blood! Didn't you never read the Varney books?'

'*S'il te plaît! Je ne suis pas un vampire! Je cherche Sheba!*' In his panic, he forgot where he was and spoke in French, the language he had grown up using.

'A Frenchie!' one of the crowd shouted.

'Throw 'im back in the Thames and let 'im swim 'ome!' said another.

'No!' The sunlight was really burning now. A scream of pain began to build up in his belly, but he forced it down and cried out in English. 'Please! Let me go! I'm just a boy – my name is Remy! But I can't stay in the sun . . . it hurts my skin!'

'Daylight 'urts 'im,' said the sailor. 'That proves it . . . 'e's not natural!'

'What are you s'posed to do with vampires, then? Chop their 'eads off?'

'Nah, you bury them at a crossroads. With a stake through their heart.'

'In China, you write out a spell in chicken's blood and stick it on their face.'

Remy could feel the flesh around his mouth begin to pucker and scorch. Soon the skin would blister and pop, then it would slide off in gobbets. It would be agony for him, and there was a good chance he might die soon after. And then so would his mother, trapped in that cellar: scared and alone and waiting for him to return.

The thought of it made him sick with fear. He

drew the deepest breath he could and let it out in a piercing scream, one that stilled the tongues of all those crowding around him. And then he shouted into the silence – one last, desperate plea . . .

'Let me go! I must find Sheba! I must find the Carnival!'

There was silence for a moment. A tiny instant in which he hoped his words had worked.

But then the sailor holding him laughed. 'A carnival? You need a carnival all right. You should be one of the exhibits! The world's smallest, crispiest vampire.'

Guffaws burst out from the twenty or so dockhands that surrounded him, loud enough to drown out Remy's sobs. The skin on his hands was bright pink now, dotted with patches of crimson that had begun to spread. The pain was almost unbearable, and the edges of his vision began to blur. Tears poured from his crimson eyes, making it worse. Through the haze he just about saw the figure of a stocky old sea captain with a threadbare pullover and tobacco-stained beard. Shouldering his way through the gawkers, he barged to the front of the group and looked up at Remy.

'Did you say Sheba, lad?' the old man asked. 'The Carnival of the Lost?'

'Yes!' Remy screamed the word, hoping it would be understood. 'Yes! Sheba!'

The next thing he knew, the old captain had pulled him from the sailor's grip and draped his woollen jumper over Remy's head. It smelt strongly of pipe smoke, sweat and old fish, but it cut out the sun's glare instantly. The searing pain stopped, leaving behind a sizzling, as if he had just been fried like a kipper.

'You come with me, laddie,' the old man said. 'Large 'Arry knows who you're after. I'll see you find your way to 'er.'

'Oi!' shouted the sailor who had grabbed him. 'That's my vampire! I caught it meself! I was going to make a fortune, showing it off in a sideshow!'

Remy could hear a growl coming from Large 'Arry's throat. 'You'll do nuffing of the sort, mate,' he said. 'This lad's under my protection, and that's the end of it.'

Whoever this Large 'Arry was, he clearly had some power on the dock. The sailor fell silent, as did all of the cheering, laughing crowd.

A gnarled old hand rested on Remy's shoulder, gently guiding him onwards, towards the cluster of sheds and warehouses he had seen earlier. He tried to move his feet and walk, but they wouldn't budge. His eyes scanned the crowd around him, his mind taunting him by painting the staring faces with panels of metal, with cogwheel teeth and spinning, iron eyes. And all the while that sound, echoing in his head: *tickticktickticktick* . . .

Was that Thom, standing on the deck? Or there, in the shadows by that crate? Had he managed to slip on to the boat after him? Was he watching him even now?

The pain, the fear, the sick worry for his mother: all of it spun around his brain like a whirlpool. His legs buckled and, for the second time that day, he fell to the dockside.

CHAPTER TWO

In which we meet some old friends.

R emy opened his eyes.

Or tried to. There was something covering his face; wet, cool and clammy. Was he drowning? Had they thrown him in the river? For a second, he panicked, reaching up to claw at his eyes, to free them so he could see. Then a tender hand closed over his and a voice spoke: gentle, polite and English.

'It's all right. Be calm. It's just a cloth and some soothing ointment. Your face was burnt by the sun. But you're indoors now, and you're safe.'

He realised he was lying down on something soft. A bed or sofa of some kind. Silk sheets covered him, and the loud noises of the docks were gone.

No chuffing of steam engines, lapping of waves or shouting sailors. Just the breeze blowing through an open window and the distant clop of horse hooves on cobblestones from outside.

'Pamplemousse!' His first thought. His blistered hands struggled on top of the blankets, trying to reach for his pocket.

'Are you looking for this?' said the voice. Something smooth was placed in his hand. He felt the familiar map of cracks and glue. His thumb found the worn spot where it had rubbed poor Pamplemousse's ear away to nothing.

'Thank you,' he croaked. Then: 'Where am I?' His throat hurt when he spoke, rubbed raw from his screaming. The skin of his face and hands throbbed as well, although he could feel they had been coated with something soothing.

'Far away from the shipyard,' the voice said. 'Far away from anyone who would hurt you. A friend of mine called Large 'Arry brought you to me. He said you were shouting my name.'

'Sheba?' Remy pawed at his eyes again, hardly daring to believe he had found her. The one person who might be able to help his mother.

'Here, let me.' The gentle hands left his and, a moment later, the cloth was peeled away. Blinking his eyes, Remy saw that he was in a clean, bright bedroom decorated with striped wallpaper and scores of framed pictures. He was lying on a four-poster bed and beside him was a woman, several years younger than his mother, with a mane of chestnut ringlets. She wore a silk shirt with a high collar and a brooch at the neck, and long, flowing skirts that billowed out from her narrow waist. She had full lips that were drawn into a pout of worry, and her eyes ... at first sight they were coppery brown, but shimmering around the irises was an orange glow. A secret fire, a wildness, hidden inside.

'Drink this,' she said, offering him a glass of water filled with chips of ice. Remy noticed her long, elegant fingers and my, what sharp nails she had ...

'*Merci*,' he said, taking a swallow. The water was so cold, it hurt his mouth, but the chill soothed his throat. Once he had taken a few sips, he lay back and examined his hands. They were covered in gloopy cream, and looked quite sore underneath. Luckily, Large 'Arry had blocked the sun with his jumper before the blistering started.

'I don't think the burns are too bad,' Sheba said. She took a hand mirror from the bedside table and held it so he could check his face.

It was also covered with cream, but he could see the pink blotches around his mouth. They stood out against his pale skin, as did the deep crimson of his eyes. Everything else was still the same: the pointed ears, the strands of lank black hair and the tips of two fangs that poked between his lips no matter how he tried to hide them. He passed the mirror back to Sheba as quickly as he could.

'Don't worry,' she said, smiling at him. 'We are all a little different here.'

'There are others?' Remy asked.

Sheba nodded and, as if on cue, footsteps sounded outside the room. The door opened and three people walked in. Remy stared at them with wide eyes.

The first was a man with stubby legs but incredibly long arms. Hunched over, he was not much taller than a child, but Remy could see he had a bushy pair of sideburns and a carefully coiffured head of hair. He also had a snub nose and a mouth full of tusks that jutted up below his wide yellow eyes.

Following was a tall, slender figure wearing a

tightly cut suit and a pair of black leather gloves. Remy thought it was a young man at first, but when he looked closer he could tell from the soft jawline and eye make-up that she was female. Seeing a woman in a suit didn't surprise him[ii] – his mother often wore a jacket and trousers – but the rest of this person's face did. She looked around eighteen or twenty, much younger than Sheba. Her eyes, ringed with black kohl, had slitted pupils, like a cat's. They glared out at him from under a mop of spiky, unruly hair and, Remy noticed, there was the trace of more fur at the edge of her cheeks and jawline. The faint hint of stripes. She moved like a wild animal, ready to pounce at any second.

The third figure shuffled along behind the others, obviously having trouble walking. His body was covered in thick, bony plates that stretched his clothes to the seams. A knobbly forehead made it hard for him to see, and he wheezed with every breath, as if each gasp was a battle.

'This is our family,' said Sheba. She pointed at the man with the tusks first. 'This is Pyewacket, my oldest friend. The young lady is Inji, and this is her brother Sil.'

'Hello,' whispered Remy, not knowing whether to feel frightened or at home. And then, remembering his manners, 'I am Remiel. Remy for short.'

'That's an unusual name,' said Sheba.

'My mother chose it,' said Remy. 'It's an angel's name. She always said I was her angel.'

'She'd have been better off calling you after a demon,' said Pyewacket. Then he winced and covered his face with his gangly hands. 'I'm sorry! That one just slipped out! I couldn't help it . . .'

'*You* can't talk, anyway,' said Inji. 'You make him look like a beauty queen. And weren't you the one who used to pretend he was a witch's imp for a living?'

'Yes, and you used to have more fur than an alley cat having a bad hair day, until Sheba taught you how to get rid of it,' said Pyewacket, with a huff. 'Anyway, that's all in the past, now. I'm going to become a gentleman detective. I decided the other day. I'm frightfully sorry if I caused you any offence, young chap.' He sketched out an elaborate bow to Remy, who had to chuckle a little.

'Ignore them, Remy,' said Sheba. 'They always bicker like this. Every day, for the best part of ten long years. Now, would you like to tell us why you were searching for me? And maybe where you are from?'

'Allow me,' said Pyewacket, barging in front of Sheba. He made a show of looking Remy up and down. He even picked up his old, filthy coat from the end of the bed and gave it a sniff.

'Hmm, let me see … pale skin with a greenish tint and a reaction to sunlight would suggest a long period of time living underground. The jacket is horribly dirty and smells of coal dust. He clutches the head of a porcelain doll, one which is missing its body.'

Pyewacket rubbed his sideburns in thought before snapping his fingers and declaring: 'This young chap has lived his life chained in a mineshaft, with only an ancient copy of a society magazine for company. The little blighter was so hungry, he had to eat most of his toy doll to survive. Then, one fateful day, he spotted Sheba's picture in the magazine, from the time when she used to gallivant around at balls and suchlike, and fell in love. He decided to crawl out and track her down. Romantic, but also a tad creepy, laddie. You should probably be ashamed of yourself.'

Remy blushed and shook his head. 'That's …

that's nothing like what happened. I don't even know what you're talking about.'

'Ha!' Inji laughed and nudged Sil, who was quietly staring at one of the prints on the wall. Pyewacket cursed and, pulling a notebook from his pocket, began to scribble furiously in it.

'Please forgive him,' said Sheba. 'He has these fads every now and then. Once he was going to be a millionaire businessman. Then it was a famous actor. A politician. A horse jockey. A mountain climber. He's been through them all.'

'*This* time I'm going to be a roaring success,' said Pyewacket with a sneer. 'I just need to work on my technique a little, that's all.'

'My mother told me to find you,' said Remy. 'She's in great danger. I had to leave her in Paris. I didn't want to, but she made me promise . . . she said you could . . . help . . .'

And then, in a sudden flood, all the tears he had been holding back since he began his long journey came pouring out at once. He sobbed and shook until his sides ached, until his eyes were empty and the cream had been washed off his cheeks into puddles on the bed sheet.

When he finally couldn't cry any more, he drew a shuddering breath and looked up. The three strange people who had just walked in were politely looking at their feet as if they hadn't noticed him bawling, but Sheba was staring at him so intensely, he shrank back against his pillows.

Then, without warning, she lurched forward and grabbed his shoulders. 'Your mother,' she said. 'What's her name? Is she French? Or does she come from here, from London?'

There was the slight trace of a growl in her voice and her eyes flashed orange fire. Remy opened his mouth to speak, but all that came out was a whimper. Finally, crossing the room in a pounce, the one called Inji reached over and pulled Sheba back, whispering in her ear. 'What's got into you? You're scaring the boy!'

Sheba blinked at him, then seemed to gain control of herself. 'Sorry. So sorry,' she muttered, before standing up and walking over to the wall. Remy could see her taking deep breaths to keep calm. Had she known his mother before he was born? Did she really care about her so deeply?

'Zara,' he said, in a quiet voice. 'Her name is Zara.'

Now it was Pyewacket's turn to gasp. 'Moonie!' he shouted. 'Your mum is Sister Moon!'

Remy nodded. 'Yes. That was the name she used when she was performing. Do you know her?'

Sheba returned to his bedside. She was holding a framed picture she had taken from the wall. With trembling fingers, she held it for him to see. It was an old, faded tintype, showing a group of sideshow performers. There was a gigantic strongman, a lady in a wide-brimmed hat and greatcoat, a gruesome boy who was obviously a young Pyewacket and a little girl whose face was covered in fur. Next to them was a sign that read 'Carnival of the Lost', and beside that was another girl that had to be his mother. She had the same long black hair, the dark glasses she always wore to hide her ebony eyes, and the familiar Bowie knives in her belt. A top hat sat at a cocky angle on her head, and she looked just a few years older than he was now.

'We grew up together,' said Sheba, her voice almost a whisper. 'That's me, with the hood and furry face. Then the horrid ogre that owned us sold her off to a show in Paris. We wrote letters for many years. She told me she had met someone, a young man, and that she was happy. We always planned to see each other again, but then the letters stopped . . .'

'The man must have been my father,' said Remy. 'He was an act at the Théâtre de Rêves, where she worked. I was born there, but soon afterwards there was an accident. My father . . . he died. After that, my mother changed. She left the theatre and took a small apartment. We lived there on our own, hidden away. I couldn't go out during the day, because of my skin, and she worked at night . . . we didn't really speak to anybody. Not ever . . . the only company I had was Pamplemousse . . .'

Sheba put her hand on his shoulder again, but this time softly, full of care. Tears were brimming in her eyes. 'Remy, I'm so sorry. I didn't know any of this. If I had . . . I would have been there for her. For you both.'

Pyewacket cleared his throat. 'You said she was in danger. Can you tell us what happened?'

Remy flinched. The very idea of talking about it made him feel like diving beneath the sheets and never coming out. But his mother was depending on him. She believed that this group of people – somehow – would be able to help her. He had to go back and relive it all. For her.

'They came one night, when my mother was out,' he said. His voice was so quiet, everyone had to crowd round the bed to hear. 'I was reading by the fire, when the door to our apartment smashed open. All five of them were there.'

'All five of who?' Inji asked.

'Them,' said Remy. 'The half-people. The ones made of machines.'

'We're going to need a bit more information than that, half-pint,' said Pyewacket.

'Describe them,' Sheba urged.

Remy closed his eyes and shuddered, but forced himself to picture them. 'There were three men and two women,' he said. 'But they weren't all there. Bits of them had gone and instead there was metal. Machinery. One had half a face. One had iron legs. The others all had one or both arms missing. There were pincers and claws and guns instead. And you could hear them ticking. Ticking all the time.'

'What did they do?' Pyewacket had his notebook out again, and was poised to scribble.

'They walked in,' said Remy, 'and they grabbed

me. They tied me up and blindfolded me. When my mother came back, she noticed the broken door. I heard her fighting with them, but they were too strong for her. She was knocked down. She was hurt . . .'

More tears welled up, but Sheba squeezed his shoulder. He could see she was crying too. 'Is she . . . is she still alive?'

Remy nodded. 'They took us to a house in the Rue Chapon. We were thrown into the cellar, in the dark. They kept coming to question my mother, asking the same things, over and over again.'

'What questions?' Sheba said. 'What did they want to know?'

Remy frowned. 'It didn't make any sense. They kept saying they worked for *L'Araignée* – the Spider – and they wanted to know where "Marie's map" was. "Where is the map? Where is the map?" they kept asking. But my mother couldn't tell them. She honestly didn't know, and she was telling the truth, I promise!'

'Marie?' Sheba leaned closer, frowning. 'Are you sure they used that name?'

'Yes,' Remy nodded. 'They said it many times.'

'I know what you're thinking, Sheebs,' said Pyewacket. 'It's probably a common French name, though ...'

Sheba's frown deepened. 'Yes,' she said. 'But still ...'

'Go on, Remy,' Pyewacket urged. 'Tell us what happened next.'

'We were there for a long time,' Remy said. 'Then one night a lady came and took me out to use the toilet. When she tied me up again, the knots were loose. I managed to slip out, to take my blindfold off, but I couldn't free my mother. She was locked up with chains and there was no key. I tried to break them, I tried so hard ...'

Sheba hugged him then, hugged him tight. 'I know you tried your best,' she said, and kissed the top of his head. Apart from his mother, nobody had ever held him like that. Nobody had even wanted to.

'She said I should go. She made me climb out of the window. She said the Carnival would help me. You will, won't you? Please say you will.'

Sheba took his face in her hands and looked at him. The amber blaze crackled in her eyes again, but this time it wasn't frightening. This time it was full of a power he knew would soon be unleashed to help free his mother.

'By my claws and teeth and fur,' Sheba said. 'I swear that we will free your mother. These people that took her have no idea what trouble they're in.'

Behind her, Pyewacket cracked his knobbly knuckles and Inji peeled off one of her leather gloves. She flexed her fingers as needle-sharp claws sprang from her fingertips.

'Nobody messes with the Carnival,' she said. And smiled.

Chapter Three

In which Remy explores the city.

Remy spent the remains of the day resting in the soft, quiet bed. He fell asleep several times: deep, restful sleep for the first time in nearly a week. Knowing that he had found help for his mother had taken some of the worry from his mind.

Every now and then, one of the Carnival brought up a tray of food for him. There was breakfast of porridge, mutton, coffee and eggs. A pie, more mutton, roast potatoes and sponge pudding for lunch. Afternoon tea was scones heaped with cream and jam, and then he had to turn away dinner because he thought he might be sick. He had never eaten so much in his life.

As evening drew on, and the sky outside began to darken, Sheba came into the room carrying a small suit of grey velvet and some crisp white shirts.

'I believe these might fit you,' she said. 'They belonged to Glyph, when he was much younger. He was about the same build as you.'

'Was he one of the Carnival too?' Remy asked.

'He still is,' said Sheba. 'You will meet him soon. He is a very busy young man these days, though. He performs stage magic and also does the odd bit of work for our friend Inspector Abernathy of Scotland Yard – helping solve crimes and other important business. I have sent word to him, to see if he knows anything about this Spider character those awful people said they were working for.'

Remy was confused. 'How would he know anything about that?'

'Well, Abernathy might. He's an important detective, you see. And Glyph is of great value to him, because he has a special Gift. It's proved very useful in catching criminals. You'll see shortly. For now, do you think you feel up to a trip? The sun has gone down, so your skin should be safe from harm.'

Remy almost leapt out of bed. Now that he had

rested, he was filled with the burning need to be doing something again. 'Are we going back to Paris? To rescue Mother?'

'Not quite yet,' said Sheba. 'There are some old friends we need to visit first.'

Remy's face fell. He thought they would be dashing into action, not calling on acquaintances for tea. But Sheba was pointing to the picture she had shown him earlier.

'That lady with the long coat. We used to call her Mama Rat, but her real name is Marie. It can only be her map that these people are after, I am certain of it, no matter what Pyewacket says. They must have discovered Sister Moon – your mother – knew her at some point.'

'So, she has the map? What is it a map of?'

Sheba shrugged. 'I'm afraid I don't know either of those things. In all the time we spent together, Mama never mentioned a map of any kind. She never really spoke about her life before the Carnival. But we need to find out. If we have what these monsters are after, we will be able to make a trade for your mother.'

Remy felt a buzz of hope. A tingle in his chest. Would it really be as easy as getting this map and then swapping it for his mother? But what could be so important it was worth kidnapping someone for?

'I'll leave you to change,' said Sheba, placing the clothes on a chair. As soon as she had left the room, Remy hopped out of bed and started pulling on the new clothes.

'This Mama Rat, Pamplemousse,' he said to the broken doll's head as it watched him from the bedside table with its one remaining eye. 'Could she really have the map the machine-people were after?' He hardly dared believe it, but the embers of hope he had been carrying since leaving Paris had begun to flare into a blaze.

Except ... every second he spent in this country was another his mother spent locked in that cellar. If they didn't get back to her quickly, it might all be too late.

The sooner they met this rat lady and were on their way to France, the better.

*

The others were gathered downstairs in the front room, dressed in dark clothing: long coats and hats that hid their faces. They looked like a group of spies about to set out on a mission.

'Ah,' said Pyewacket, as he entered. 'Here he is. Looking all afternoonified.[iii] Are you ready for a visit to one of London's most secret sights?'

'Where are we going?' Remy asked, his voice shaking a little. He wasn't used to walking around outside, especially in a strange city. His ten years of life had mostly been spent in his small apartment, or sitting on the rooftop balcony, looking down at the street lights below.

'Mama Rat is part of a troupe of performers called the Scarlequins,' said Inji. 'They are Gifted, like us, but they ran away from their shows and circuses. Now they choose to perform for themselves.'

'It is hard to discover where their next show will be,' said Sheba. 'Unless you have ears in the right places.'

Pyewacket grinned, making his large, jug-handle ears wiggle. 'And what's best is that they always do their shows in the most unusual hideaways.'

All this was making Remy even more nervous. His mother had rarely spoken about the Théâtre de Rêves – the sideshow where she and his father had met – but when she did, he could tell her memories of it were bad ones. And the way she had kept him hidden away all his life: he knew it was because she was frightened that he would end up in such a place. Anyone who was *different* like them always did.

'They won't ... they won't try and make *us* perform, will they?' he said.

Pyewacket laughed, but Sheba's face was deadly serious. 'Not while I'm there to look after you,' she said. 'But the Marquess – the person who runs the Scarlequins – is one to be wary of. Don't speak to her unless one of us is with you.'

Remy gulped, but Inji took his hand and squeezed. She looked down at him with those kohl-rimmed eyes, the pupils now wide and almost round. 'Don't you worry, little one,' she said. 'Anybody who tries to hurt you will have to go through me first.'

Remy smiled back at her, grateful. But he couldn't help thinking about the five servants of the Spider, with their mechanical bodies. Fierce as Inji was, he didn't think even *she* would be a match for them.

*

A carriage came for them shortly after. Gleaming black, with tall wheels, leather seats and velvet curtains, it was pulled by four stomping horses and driven by a man in a long leather coat and top hat. As they left the house and climbed inside, Remy couldn't help but marvel at the lives this Carnival lived. He had always thought people like them, who didn't fit with what society called 'normal', had to be sad, lonely creatures, scraping to get by. Either that, or be put on show and stared at like monsters.

These folks lived in a perfect house and drove around in carriages, like the rich and glamorous aristocrats he used to watch from his balcony in Montmartre. He had always dreamed about what it would be like, riding along the boulevards, visiting the theatre and bistros; having friends to laugh and joke with, without worrying what they thought of his face.

'Here,' said Sheba. 'Why don't you sit by the window? We can give you a tour of London on the way.'

Remy clambered on to the wide seat and knelt so he could see through the glass. Sil took the seat opposite him, and peered through his own window as well. The street outside was full of tall houses, brightly lit by gas lamps inside. He could see families sitting down to supper, maids and cooks working in the kitchen, children laughing with their brothers and sisters.

'How is it you all live here?' He asked the question without thinking, and then realised it was probably quite rude.

'We're lucky enough to know Her Ladyship there,' said Pyewacket, pointing at Sheba. 'She's related to lords and ladies, you know. She owns the house and has an estate and everything.'

Sheba blushed, and poked Pyewacket with the end of her parasol. 'My family was slightly wealthy,' she explained. 'Although I never knew them. I didn't find out about them until I was around your age, and they were long dead by then. I had a relative who helped me get my inheritance and become free of the Carnival life.'

'But you call yourselves the Carnival?' Remy frowned. 'Do you still perform shows?'

Inji laughed. 'Not any more. We help people like ourselves. We try to make their lives a bit better.

Glyph, our friend, has his magic show and works for Scotland Yard. It all brings in a bit of extra money. We're able to live pretty well.'

'The name reminds us of where we came from,' said Sheba. 'We never want to forget the hardship and poverty we had to endure, like so many in this city still do. And we have also grown quite attached to it.' She lifted her parasol and banged on the roof three times with the handle. With a crunch of wheels and clatter of hooves, the carriage moved off down the road.

*

They drove alongside the river, heading east. Remy could see the wide expanse of water in between the rows of warehouses he had been desperately trying to hide in that very morning. It was choked with ships of all sizes, their masts stretching up to block his view of the north bank.

Soon, they turned towards the Thames and pulled on to a wide, stone bridge. They rattled on to it, mixing with a thick stream of traffic. More carriages, two-wheeled hansom cabs, wagons piled high with

crates and barrels, and omnibuses: double-decked buses packed full of passengers, all heaved along by teams of tired-looking horses.

On one side, Remy could see the dome of a white stone building. From what his mother had told him, he guessed it must be St Paul's Cathedral. It rose up from among a forest of other roofs and chimneys. Brick buildings as tall and thickly clustered as those in Paris. He was used to looking out across such a sea of stone and smoke from the hill of Montmartre, but it was another thing, being down among all the noise and bustle.

'This is London Bridge,' said Sheba. 'It once had houses built high on either side, and waterwheels under its arches.'

'And don't forget all the heads on spikes over the gate,' said Pyewacket. 'You never get to see a good spiked head any more.'

Remy shivered.

The carriage nudged its way across the bridge and on to the other side of the river, where it turned in among a maze of wide roads. There were shop fronts on either side, and pavements full of people. In the glow of gas street lights, Remy could see hundreds of them: tall gentlemen with top hats and walking canes; ladies with wide, streaming skirts and hats adorned with feathers and lace. There were shabbier figures as well: tinkers and traders smeared with grime, selling odds and ends from street stalls or baskets; young lads carrying advertising boards, or brooms to sweep the muck from the cobbles. And – hidden in the shadows of doorways – glimpses of skeleton-thin children, huddled against their mothers under tattered scraps of sacking, their hands reaching out for a penny or two to stop them from starving. Every layer of London society flashed by the carriage window in seconds, as they rattled past on the cobbles.

Finally, they came to a halt outside an immense slab of a building, with a stone portico on its front – a triangle full of carved statues, supported by a row of columns, as if it was an ancient Greek temple.

'This is Mansion House,' said Inji, as she opened the carriage door and swung down the steps to climb out.

'Is this where the show is?' Remy asked, suddenly feeling very underdressed.

'No, you plum,' Pyewacket laughed. 'This is

where the Mayor of London lives. *He* wouldn't be seen dead at a Scarlequin gig.'

Remy hopped out and stood on the pavement, while they all waited for Sil to clamber down. Remy brushed his hair forward, to cover his pointed ears and hide his face, but the folk passing by were too busy talking among themselves to notice him. Still, being near so many complete strangers made him nervous. He half expected to hear one of them *ticktickticking* ... the noise of clockwork getting steadily louder until one of his mechanical captors leapt out of the crowd and grabbed him. His fingers found Pamplemousse in his pocket and he rubbed the doll's smooth edges for comfort.

'It's dark. It's safe. No one can see us,' he whispered.

He could feel the press of cool shadows all around, soothing him, healing his skin. Without even thinking, he drew them tighter, using them to blur the edges of his shape, to make him blend in with the gloom.

'All set,' said Sheba, when Sil was standing next to them and the carriage had pulled away. 'Where's Remy, though?'

'I'm still here,' he said, letting his shroud of shadows slip. The others jumped, as he suddenly appeared again.

'That's a good trick,' said Inji. 'You'll have to teach me some day.'

'You won't be able to learn that,' said Pyewacket. 'That's a Gift from his mother, that is. Sister Moon: daughter of the dark. Looks like you're a chip off the old block, little one.'

As if in an attempt to follow his example, they all pulled their coats and hats tight around them and merged with the stream of people walking past the mansion.

*

Turning the corner, they headed down a quieter street, full of four-storey buildings. The side of Mansion House, with its rows and rows of ornate windows, seemed to go on for ever. It was followed by a narrow church, with a tall, white steeple, and then they were among Georgian townhouses and muck-spattered cobblestones.

'This is Walbrook,' said Sheba. 'There's a river

running underneath our feet right now, heading down to the Thames.'

Remy looked at the cobbles, expecting them to crack open and plunge him into the water below.

'Don't panic,' said Pyewacket. 'Old Walbrook is trapped inside the brick pipes of the sewer system. What's left of it anyway. London's swallowed up all of its ancient rivers. Apart from the big one, of course.'

Halfway down the street they paused outside a shabby building. The stonework was blackened with soot, the windowpanes cracked and loose in their frames. It looked more like the venue for a murder than an impressive, secret show.

But, as Remy watched, several people walked up the street and stopped at the doorway. After they had knocked and whispered a few words, the front door swung open and swallowed them up. Something was happening inside.

'Here we are, my beauties,' said Pyewacket, baring his tusks in a wide grin. He hopped up the steps and tapped out an odd rhythm on the chipped paintwork of the door. With a creak, it opened a fraction, and an eye peeped out.

'Yes?'

'We're here for the show,' said Pyewacket, puffing out his chest. And then, suddenly remembering, he added: 'The password is "Muffins".'

'Sorry,' came a deep voice. 'We don't let in jelly-brained idiots.'

Pyewacket blinked his round yellow eyes. 'But . . . but that's the password! I paid good money for that!'

'Even if it was,' said the voice. 'I can't let you in. You smell like a rhino's toilet parts. It would make the whole audience bring up their supper.'

'*What?!* How dare you!' Pyewacket hopped up and down with rage. He lifted his long arms to pound on the door, when it swung open anyway. The sound of booming laughter came from inside.

As Remy and the rest of the Carnival walked up the steps, they saw who was making all the noise. It was a colossal man, with muscles like boulders, bent over double, chuckling until he cried. His head was covered with silver stubble and etched deep with masses of scars. He wore a greatcoat over a black-and-white striped jersey, and was pointing at Pyewacket, who was now beginning to sulk.

'Gigantus,' said Pye. 'That was hilarious. I bet you're very proud of yourself now.'

'I am,' the big man wheezed. 'Your *face* ...'

'Lucky for you, I am now a gentleman,' said Pyewacket. 'A less civilised person might have called you a fat, dim-witted goon, or something equally rude.'

Remy wondered what was going on, and was even more surprised when Sheba rushed up the steps and wrapped her arms around the giant man, squeezing him tight. Then he remembered the picture from the wall: this enormous creature had been in the original Carnival. The one his mother was a part of.

'Come here, you fool,' Gigantus was saying. He grabbed Pyewacket and hugged him as well. Then he nodded to Inji and Sil.

'This is Remy,' said Sheba, when she had prised herself away. 'He's Sister Moon's son.'

'Well, I never,' said Gigantus. He knelt, and put out a hand that was bigger than Remy's entire head. 'I knew your mother well. How is she?'

Remy tried to answer, but all that came out was a squeak.

'She's in trouble,' said Sheba. 'That's why we're here. We need to speak to Mama Rat.'

Gigantus nodded. 'Anything to help Moon. Come

on in,' he said. 'I'll make sure Marie sees you after the show.' He stood back, beckoning them into the house and down the hall. It looked dark and deserted inside, all bare floorboards and peeling wallpaper.

'Aren't you performing?' Inji asked, as they filed past. Gigantus shook his head.

'My back isn't what it was, these days,' he said. 'I mostly man the door now. And throw out anyone who causes trouble.' He gave Pyewacket a stern look, and then laughed once more. 'Enjoy the performance, everyone.'

Leaving the big man standing at the doorway, they walked down the dingy corridor, into the gloom of the abandoned house.

CHAPTER FOUR

In which the Scarlequins
perform another secret show.

Following the corridor, they found themselves in a pitch-dark, unlit kitchen. It had been stripped of everything except a large porcelain sink and a couple of wonky shelves.

'This can't be right,' said Pyewacket. 'Where's all the lights and bunting and everything?'

'Look,' said Inji. Her cat-eyes were made for the dark, and she spotted it first: the joker from a pack of pasteboard playing cards, pinned to a door frame on the far side of the room. When she walked across and opened the door, there was a steep flight of stairs behind, heading down into a dark, dark cellar.

'After you, Remy,' said Pyewacket, giving him a gentle shove. 'The night is your thing, after all.'

Hoping that wasn't another vampire joke, Remy edged closer to the steps. Thankfully, Inji took his hand, and the pair of them went down together.

He expected to emerge into an underground circus ring, full of clowns and acrobats, but the cellar was as dim and empty as the room above.

'Where to now?' he whispered, as the others followed down the steps.

'There's another card,' said Inji, pointing to the far corner. Halfway down the wall hung a sheet of tarpaulin, the joker pinned on to a corner. All around it were discarded bricks, pulled out and tumbled into stacks. There was mortar dust and dirt everywhere, as if the place was a building site.

'I know the Scarlequins like weird venues, but this is ridiculous,' said Pyewacket. He huffed across and lifted the tarpaulin sheet, releasing a flood of light, which blazed into the cellar.

A large hole had been dug through the wall, revealing a secret underground space, built over and hidden goodness knows how many years ago.

Remy's curiosity burned away his nerves, and he dashed over and peered inside.

The lights were the first thing he noticed: strings of candles in glass jam jars, hanging from the low ceiling inside. There was a bubble of noise, the chatter of many excited voices, and a wall of sticky heat. Once his sensitive eyes had adjusted, he climbed through the hole and dropped down three feet or so to stand on a floor of packed mud.

It was a temple. An entire temple, from some distant age and religion, buried beneath the London streets.

There were two rows of columns stretching down its length to an altar at the end. Lumps of roughly hewn stone made up the outside walls, but only some of them were visible. The rest were hidden behind banks of earth, from which shards of masonry and pieces of broken pot poked. Most of the place was still buried, nestled inside the soil that had risen up around it over thousands of years.

In front of the altar, sitting on benches made of crates, planks and pieces of shattered stonework, were thirty or so people – the source of all the hubbub. And in front of them – framed by a pair of dirty, patchwork curtains – was what presumably was the stage.

'Look at this place,' Sheba gasped, climbing through the hole to stand beside him. 'It must be Roman! A lost temple from the first days of London.'

'Londinium, it was actually called,' said a voice. 'This was a temple to Mithras. A secret religion, even then. It once sat on the banks of the River Walbrook, right in the heart of the city.'

Striding over to them was a tall figure, a woman in a long frock coat made from diamonds of patchwork leather. She had pale white skin, silver hair that spilled over her shoulders and eyes like chips of moonbeams.

'Marquess,' said Sheba.

The woman bowed from the waist, twirling her hands. When she looked up, she was smiling. 'A visit from the Carnival,' she said. 'I *am* honoured.'

Sheba held out a handful of coins, which the Marquess swiftly pocketed. She nodded to Pyewacket and Inji, who were helping Sil clamber in through the hole.

And then her eyes fell on Remy.

'You have a new member,' she said, bending over

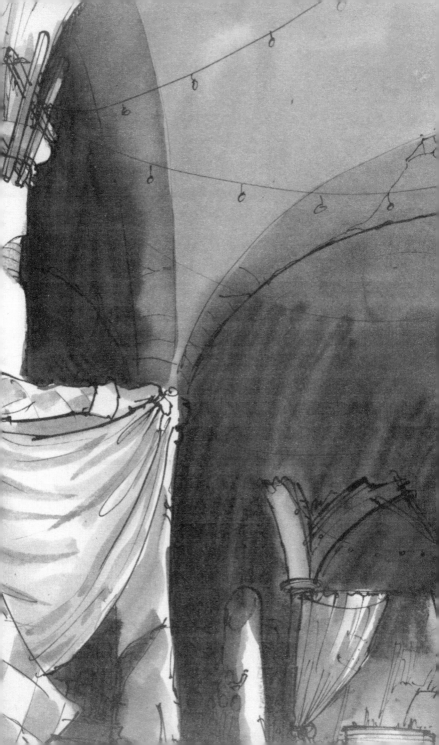

to peer at him. A strange expression ghosted over her face, chasing away the smile that had been there a moment before. 'Do . . . do I know you?'

'This is Sister Moon's son,' said Sheba. She drew Remy closer to her with a protective hand. 'I don't believe you had the honour of meeting her, so I can't see how you can possibly recognise him.'

'But I *have* seen him before,' said the Marquess. 'Or perhaps I have dreamed of him . . .'

'Come, Remy,' said Sheba. 'Let us find our seats.'

She led him past the Marquess, who still stared at Remy as she rubbed her chin with the long fingers of one hand. The others followed, and they picked their way through lumps of mud and patches of tiled floor to find seats among the audience.

'What was all that about?' Pyewacket asked, once they were seated, backs up against the muddy wall.

'Who knows?' Sheba replied. 'That Marquess is a weird one. She doesn't look a day older than when we first saw her, and that must have been fifteen years ago. Some say she's as old as London itself.'

'She gives me the creeps,' said Inji. 'Here, Remy – do you want to sit on my lap? You'll be able to see better.'

Remy gave a shy nod, and moved across so Inji could hoist him on to her knees. He lifted Pamplemousse out of his pocket, so he could see too. It felt strange, being so close to someone who wasn't his mother, but Inji was strong and brave, like her. And he liked the way she smelt of lavender.

Next to him, Sil gave a little grunt – the first noise Remy had heard him make – as the lights in the temple lowered and the tatty curtains drew open.

The audience hushed as the Marquess strode on to the stage. She welcomed them all, and told them about the amazing spectacles they were about to witness. The audience gasped and cooed at everything she said, and for the first time Remy noticed that they weren't all fine ladies and gentlemen, as he might have expected, but poor street folk dressed in battered hats and threadbare clothes. Many had missing arms or legs, and some carried the bowls and pots they used for begging on the streets. He wondered how they could afford to be here. Or were the Scarlequins performing for free?

He was about to ask Inji, but then the first act came on, and thoughts of anything else left his mind.

It was a grizzled old soldier, dressed in his army redcoat. He made a show of marching back and forth, drawing his military sabre and swishing it through the air. *This isn't very impressive*, Remy thought, but then – to his horror – the soldier lifted his sword, put the point in his mouth and swallowed the whole thing to the hilt.

Everyone cheered, then cheered again as the Marquess handed him another to swallow. And another, and another. Soon he had the handles of five swords poking from his mouth. Remy had visions of the poor chap's insides being sliced up like chopped beef, but he somehow managed to stay alive. He even managed to bow before walking, rather stiffly, off stage.

Next was a young girl with eyes of pure gold. She threw knives, cleavers and darts at a range of targets, always hitting the bullseye. Even when she was blindfolded.

A lady came on who could fold herself into a tiny wooden box. A young man stuck pins through his arms and cheeks and didn't seem to feel any pain. On and on it went, each act more marvellous than the last.

'Good, isn't it?' Pyewacket whispered to him, in between turns.

'It's ... amazing,' said Remy. 'Is this what my mother used to do?'

'Yes,' said Pyewacket. 'We all did. Sister Moon used to snuff out the lights, then dash across the room, picking everyone's pocket in a heartbeat. Gigantus used to lift anything and everything. And I was a witch's imp.'

'Basically, you just sat there looking ugly,' said Inji, snickering.

'What did you do?' Remy asked her, turning around on her lap.

Inji shrugged. 'I joined the Carnival nine years ago, after they had stopped performing. But Sil and I were put on show, many times. I used to turn into a wildcat and climb the walls, and the audience used to throw bottles at poor Sil's head.'

Sil groaned at the thought, and Inji reached over to rub his knee.

'And Sheba?' Remy said. 'What was her act?'

Pyewacket simply gave him a wink. 'Maybe you'll find out, one day,' he said. 'Just make sure you're standing well clear when it happens.'

The crowd began to cheer before he could say any more, and the last act came on. It was a lady with long grey hair, hanging down beneath a broad-brimmed hat. She wore a greatcoat and trousers, tucked into leather boots. Even though she was much older, Remy recognised her from the picture in Sheba's house. It was Mama Rat – Marie – the one whose map might just save his mother's life.

*

Remy watched as Mama Rat brought out a large wooden box and began to open various doors on it. Within a few minutes, the whole thing had unfolded into a miniature circus, painted in bright lozenges of red and yellow. Then, from under chairs and out of holes in the walls, a group of plump black and brown rats scurried. They clambered up on to the model circus and began doing handstands, riding unicycles and tightrope-walking.

It would have been an amazing sight, but all Remy could think of was the map. He stared at the woman, willing the performance to end, so they could speak to her – find out if she really was the mysterious 'Marie' and, if so, whether she had a map. All the magic of this hidden place, this secret show, vanished. In fact, he felt guilty for even sitting here, enjoying himself, while those mechanical brutes were probably torturing his mother right now.

Hurry up, hurry up! He forced his thoughts across the chamber, trying to control Mama Rat like he did the night. He even wondered if he might be able to use his ability to snuff out all the candles in the room, plunging them into darkness and ending the show early. But he was not that powerful, worse luck. He could just about fold enough shadow to hide himself.

Finally, after what seemed like hours, Mama and her rodent performers took a bow and the audience began to roar with applause. Someone even threw some flowers made of folded newspaper scraps on to the stage.

The Marquess stepped out and opened to say farewell, calling all the acts out for another bow. Remy was jiggling around at this point, just wanting them to get it all over with.

'Do you need the toilet, or something?' Inji whispered in his ear.

'No,' Remy blushed. 'I just want to speak to the rat lady. To see if she has the map.'

Inji nodded. 'Won't be long now,' she said. The crowd were beginning to stand and pick their way through the piles of mud and masonry to the exit. Some of the performers came out and started taking down the lights and curtains, and Mama Rat carefully folded away her circus into its box, then waited for her pets to scamper inside. When that was done, she walked over to the Carnival and Remy, who was hopping up and down with impatience.

'My friends,' she said, her voice soft but husky, the result of many years of pipe-smoking. 'So good to see you.'

She wrapped Sheba in a tight hug, then did the same to Pyewacket. Inji shook her hand and she waved at Sil, who blinked, then looked away. Then she knelt down to be at Remy's level and gave him a broad smile.

'Gigantus told me who you are,' she said. 'Your mother was a very dear friend of mine. Just tell me what I can do to help.'

'I need the map,' Remy blurted out, then felt bad

when he saw the look of shock that crossed this kind woman's face.

'The what?' she said. 'What did you just say?'

'Perhaps we should explain first,' said Sheba. 'Maybe somewhere a bit more private?'

'I know a place,' said Mama Rat. 'Besides, we need to pack the show away and brick up the wall quick sharp. The owners of the house don't even know this is down here.'

'You mean, somebody lives in that house up there?' Pyewacket said. 'And we just strolled through it?'

'They haven't moved in yet,' said Mama Rat. 'But we still shouldn't hang about. Follow me.'

With a nod to the Marquess (who was still staring thoughtfully at Remy), Mama Rat led them all back up and on to the street. Gigantus had just seen the last of the audience out, and decided to tag along with them.

'There's a coffee shop just around the corner,' said Mama Rat, leading them down Walbrook, towards the river. 'It's always empty this time of night. And I know the owner.'

They walked on to a narrow street that was

squashed end to end with shops. A sign on the corner house said it was called Budge Row.

'In here,' said Mama Rat, opening the door of a snug little café. A tiny place, with only a handful of tables, it was empty, just as she had said it would be. An elderly woman in an apron was polishing the counter as they walked in. Mama Rat gave her a nod, and she set about brewing them all some coffee.

'It's so good to see you again,' said Sheba, as they pulled out chairs and sat around a table. 'Though I wish it were in happier circumstances. Without Sister Moon being in danger.'

'Tell me everything,' said Mama Rat. Her green eyes twinkled in the light from the gas lamps on the wall as Sheba spoke, recounting everything Remy had told her earlier about his capture and what the machine-people had said. Throughout it all he could hear Gigantus quietly growling, like an angry guard dog.

'And you're certain . . . absolutely *certain* . . . they were asking for "Marie's map"?' Mama Rat frowned at Remy from under the brim of her hat. He nodded. There was no mistaking what they had said.

'Then it can only mean one thing,' said Mama Rat, with a heavy sigh. 'I thought I might never hear of that cursed thing again. There was only one other person alive, besides me, who knew about it. If this Spider is after it, then they must have made him talk somehow. And I bet it wasn't pleasant.'

'Let me guess . . . I mean *deduce*,' said Pyewacket, clearing his throat. 'It's a map of ingredients for a potion of eternal youth? No – clearly not, otherwise you wouldn't look like an old grandma. What about instructions for the most delicious pork pie in existence?'

'Ignore him,' said Sheba, rolling her eyes. 'His latest thing is pretending to be a detective. And pork pie? Is that the best you can come up with?'

'I thought it was quite good, actually,' said Pyewacket, poking out his tongue.

'Please,' said Remy. 'Whatever the map is . . . may we have it? If we can give it to these people, they might set my mother free . . .'

Mama Rat gently took hold of one of his hands. 'I'm afraid it's not here. It is safely hidden away – in Paris, as it happens. I can tell you where it is, if it would help Sister Moon, but unfortunately I cannot set foot on French soil again. You will have to find it yourselves.'

Inji was shaking her head. 'Secret maps? Gangs of villains? Staying clear of France? What's all this about? If we knew half the story, we might have a clue about what we were doing.'

Mama Rat took a moment to look around the room, to peer through the grubby windows to the street outside. Then, when she was certain it was safe to speak, she took a long-stemmed pipe out from her jacket and lit the bowl with a match.

'It's a long story,' she said, through a cloud of smoke. 'But I think you had better hear it from the start.'

CHAPTER FIVE

In which we learn about Mama Rat's secret past.

'Y ou may find this hard to believe,' she began, 'but I am actually French. I was born in the town of Dieppe, on the north coast of France.

'My parents were simple bakers. They owned a tiny boulangerie, where they worked their fingers to the bone, baking bread and trying to scrape by. They were normal, as far as I knew, and I thought I was too, right up until the day our shop had an infestation of rats.

'My father was horrified – rodents in the flour could ruin his entire business. But I found myself drawn to them. I would sit with my ear pressed to the wall; listening to their skittering and scufflings, imagining I could understand what they were saying.

'And then, one day, I could! The squeaking and snuffling somehow became thoughts in my head. Not words, as such, but images and ideas. Animals don't think in language as we do, of course.

'After that, the rats became my friends. I got to know them all by the names I gave them, and they would visit me at night. I told them where my father had placed traps, so they could avoid them, and I brought them little scraps of pastry to nibble. I thought, if I could stop them getting into the bakery's flour stores, my parents might not notice them any more, and we could all live in peace.

'Perhaps my plan might have worked, but it was not meant to be. One of them, a young brown rat I had named Beatrice, made the mistake of falling asleep on my pillow one night. My mother happened to come in, spotted Beatrice, and screamed the house down. My father was horrified – that the rats still remained, but also that I had made pets of them. He vowed to exterminate them all and, no matter how much I cried and begged, he kept his word.

'He bought a terrier dog and three cats to hunt

them, he ripped the plaster from the walls to expose their nests, he spent every spare penny he had on traps and poison. One by one, every member of the rat family was destroyed. And, in the end, my father was too. Nobody would buy his bread, for fear of getting rats' diseases. The bakery was ruined, his savings were gone. We had to pack up and take to the road.

'Of course, he blamed me for his bad luck. I spent a miserable few months, living in hovels and being shouted at all day while my empty stomach rumbled, and then I slipped away one night and stole a ride in a wagon heading for Paris.'

Pyewacket gave a snort. 'I bet you found plenty of rats to be chums with *there*,' he said.

Mama Rat smiled. 'I certainly did. The more people there are, the more rats you'll find. I soon had my first little troupe of ratties, and they helped teach me some new tricks. I've told very few people this . . . but when I am connected to a rat, I can *see* out of its eyes. I can *hear* everything it hears. A very useful Gift, and one in much demand, as I soon found out.

'I spent my first few weeks as a Parisian living

homeless on the streets. I was only a young girl, and it was no place for someone as innocent and helpless as me. But I soon discovered that I could use my talents to make a living. I made my rats dance and somersault in a little show, which earned me a few centimes. And I also had a knack for finding objects that people had lost. My rats had wonderful noses and sharp eyes. They always came scurrying back with whatever they were looking for.

'It was this trick that got me noticed by a cruel man named LeClair. At first, he charmed me with promises of a luxurious room to live in. He took me to eat in fine cafés, bought me dresses and bonbons, made me promises of riches and houses and a horse and carriage of my own ... I'm ashamed to say I was taken in, my dears. But I was young then, and foolish. Heads are easily turned when they don't know any better.

'I started working for him, using my rats to listen in on conversations in posh buildings. To spy on meetings down shady alleyways and in hidden cellars. I'd like to say I didn't know what I was doing, but I had a hunch that it was wrong. I did it anyway, though – anything to get off the streets. To have clean clothes and food that hadn't been scraped from a gutter.

'LeClair was using the information to blackmail people, you see. Once I had reported back to him, then he went and told folk that he was on to them. If they wanted him to keep quiet, they had to pay him money.

'Mostly, it was gangsters and crooked businessmen he preyed on, which somehow made it seem less bad. Then one day he had me spy on a poor restaurant owner. I discovered his secret, and LeClair used it to take all his life savings. The chap was ruined, like my own father had been after his battle against the rats.

'I refused to help him after that. But he wouldn't take no for an answer. He began to hurt my pets, pulling their tails and threatening to cut off their ears. Forcing me to work for him if I wanted to save their lives.

'I had no choice but to carry on. Although it wasn't long before LeClair picked the wrong target. He used me to spy on one of the noblemen of King Louis Philippe's court: the Marquis D'Aramon. Now *that* was a man even more cruel and evil than LeClair himself.'

'I thought the French didn't have kings,' said Inji. 'Didn't they have a revolution and get rid of them?'

'They did,' said Mama Rat. 'And they became a Republic. Then an Empire. Then they went back to having a king for a bit. Then they were a Republic for a few more years. And then they changed their minds twenty or so years ago and went back to being an Empire. I expect they'll switch again, someday.'[iv]

'That's if they don't get taken over by the Prussians[v] first,' said Gigantus. 'They're at war[vi] with them now, aren't they? And I hear it's going very badly.'

All eyes turned to Remy, but he shrugged. Apart from reading the odd newspaper and hearing cheering in the streets, he didn't know much about the fighting. There had been fanfares and celebration when the flamboyant French army marched out the month before, but he hadn't heard anything since. It was all happening far away from Paris, it seemed. Little did he know how much that was about to change.

'Well, anyway,' Mama Rat continued. 'Louis Philippe was king at the time, and D'Aramon was one of his spymasters. Which meant I soon became one of his spies, once he discovered that it was *me* who LeClair had used to eavesdrop on him.'

'What happened to LeClair?' Sheba asked.

Mama Rat shuddered. 'I don't know exactly. He just disappeared – probably ended up at the bottom of the Seine[vii] –or somewhere worse. And I found myself moved to new apartments, along with my rats, and reporting for duty in the Hôtel de Ville.

'And that quickly became my life. D'Aramon would give me a target – sometimes in Paris, sometimes in Berlin or London or Madrid – and I would be whisked off. I would have to pose as an elegant French aristocrat, attending balls or the opera in silk dresses and tiaras. Meanwhile, my rats would be hidden under the floorboards or in the walls, and I would be listening in on the conversations of politicians, noblemen … even royalty, sometimes.'

'Blimey,' said Inji. 'That's a far cry from appearing in a sideshow in a buried Roman temple.'

'It was a far cry from anything I'd ever known. I was just a poor baker's daughter, after all, my dear. But I took to it quickly. It was easy, really – pretending to be someone else. I suppose I thought it was all a bit of a game.

'Until the day D'Aramon gave me a new target: a little old lady who lived above a patisserie in the Rue Montorgueil.'

'She doesn't sound like royalty,' said Inji.

'She wasn't.' Mama Rat shook her head. 'She was just a poor old woman, struggling to get by on the few francs she had left. Or so I thought, at first.

'I got myself a job in the patisserie below where she lived, and gradually befriended her. I started off by sneaking her rum babas and éclairs when I was on my lunch break. Soon, I was being invited to have dinner with her. I listened to all her stories, helped her with the housework … she was very lonely, you see. No family. No husband. I almost went back to D'Aramon and told him there was nothing interesting about her.

'But my ratties were also spying on her the whole time. One night – after she had drunk too much wine – they heard her talking to herself about a secret. About something she must never tell, never touch, even though it could make her rich.

'As soon as I knew she *was* hiding something, it

was only a matter of time until I wheedled it out of her. It turned out she had once been a lady's maid. And not just any maid at that … she had worked in the Royal Court, for Marie Antoinette herself.'

'Is she the one who got her head chopped off?' Pyewacket asked.

'The very same,' said Mama Rat. 'She was guillotined, along with her husband King Louis the sixteenth. But before all that happened, she was involved in a scandal. Have you ever heard of the Queen's Necklace?'

The Carnival all shook their heads, although the phrase sounded familiar to Remy. Perhaps he had read it in a history book or newspaper.

'Well,' Mama Rat began to explain. 'It all happened a long time ago. Around 1780, I believe. The old lady was just a young girl then, working for the royal family at the Palace of Versailles. She was honest and hardworking, honoured to have secured herself such a good position.

'But she had an aunt who was a scheming criminal. A lady named Jeanne de la Motte. This aunt was pretending to be a countess, a noblewoman, and had tricked a very important man named the

Cardinal de Rohan into believing her. She also fooled him into thinking that she knew Queen Marie Antoinette herself.

'Of course, it was all a pack of lies. But La Motte had a plan, you see. She had heard about a Parisian jeweller who had made the most beautiful necklace ever created. It had six hundred and forty-seven enormous diamonds in it, and was worth millions of livres. They had made it for the previous king, Louis the fifteenth, who had died before he could pay for it. Now they were desperate to sell it.

'La Motte decided to trick both the jeweller *and* the cardinal. She convinced the poor man that the queen was in love with him, and that he should buy her the necklace as a present.

'How did she do this? Well, she wrote him lots of fake letters from the queen, for a start. But to do that, she needed some samples of her handwriting. And that was where the old lady, her maid, came in.

'Her crooked aunt persuaded her to steal some papers from Marie Antoinette's rooms. She was too young to know it, but once she had done that, of course, she was guilty of a serious crime.

'The letters worked, the cardinal was fooled. He

gave his money to the jeweller, and the necklace was given to La Motte, to deliver to the queen.'

'Let me guess,' said Inji. 'It never got to her.'

'Of course not,' said Mama Rat. 'It was broken up and sold off – or so La Motte claimed – and then the criminals were all caught and arrested.'

'Even the maid? The old lady?' Remy said. For some reason, he had begun to feel sorry for her.

'No,' Mama Rat smiled. 'Her part remained unknown. The biggest mystery of all, because the necklace wasn't really sold off, La Motte hid it and . . .'

'I've got it!' Pyewacket shouted. 'Her crooked aunt left her a map that leads to a map . . . '

'Why would you have a map that leads to another map, you dolt?' Inji gave Pyewacket a dig in the ribs with her elbow.

'Yes. Quite,' said Mama Rat. 'And now you've ruined the story. The old lady had a map, of course, but it was just to where the necklace was hidden.'

'And in all those years, she never thought to use it?' Sheba asked. 'She lived in poverty, knowing she could have been rich?'

'She was terrified, poor thing,' said Mama Rat.

'La Motte was executed for her crime, and if her niece let on that she had been a part of it . . . well, she would have died too. Either that or spent the rest of her life in the worst prison imaginable.'

'What happened when she told you her story?' Remy asked. 'Did she give you the map?'

Mama Rat puffed on her pipe for a good minute before answering. When she spoke, her voice was heavy with sorrow. 'No. No, she couldn't quite bear to reveal the whole secret she had kept for so long. If only she had.

'I'm ashamed to say that I reported all this to D'Aramon. I was too afraid of what might happen to me or my rats if I didn't. And I thought it was government business – for the good of my country, not just to line a greedy man's pockets.

'D'Aramon went straight to the old woman's apartment, taking a group of his thugs along with him. As soon as I found out, I dashed there myself, only to find the entire place smashed to matchwood. All her furniture, all her keepsakes, lying in pieces on the floor.

'The poor lady – it literally broke her heart – she dropped dead there and then. And standing over her, the map in his hand, was D'Aramon. He was laughing with joy, joking about how he would become the richest man in France.

'I couldn't let that happen. I sent my rats jumping and scratching at his face, then I snatched the map from him and ran. His agents hounded me all over Paris.

'I was tempted to burn the map immediately, but now I was in danger, I knew it might be the only thing that could save me if I was caught. I could trade it for my freedom.

'So I had to keep it squirrelled away somewhere safe. I had just managed to hide the cursed thing, when D'Aramon cornered me and had me thrown into prison to think about my actions. He planned to torture me to find its hiding place. I think he was going to hurt me, whether I told him or not.'

'And that's where I came in,' said Gigantus, with a grin. 'I was in the very next cell.'

'What did they lock you up for?' Pyewacket asked. 'Being too ugly?'

'I look like the Mona Lisa, compared to you,' said Gigantus. 'No, I had been doing a spot of pit-fighting. It was how I earned my crust in those days. I won every fight I was in, although sometimes the losers weren't too happy about it ...'

'Did Gigantus break you out?' Inji asked. 'Did he smash down the walls so you could escape?'

'Not quite,' said Mama Rat, smiling at the memory. 'My rats brought me the keys. I figured I could use a bit of protection, so I let this big lump out as well. He's been by my side ever since.'

'This D'Aramon was still after her,' Gigantus explained. 'I grew up here in London, so I knew it was the perfect place to hide away. We joined Plumpscuttle's sideshow, knowing that we'd fit right in. The rest of the story you're familiar with, I'm sure.'

'And you never thought to find the necklace yourself?' Pyewacket stared at her, eyes boggling. 'All that time we were working for Plumpscuttle: starving, shivering, miserable ... you could have gone and fetched it and bought us Buckingham Palace to live in!'

'Money doesn't make you happy,' said Mama Rat. 'Just look at what happened to everyone who wanted that necklace. It doomed the lot of them.'

'I wouldn't mind being doomed if I lived in a palace,' Pyewacket muttered, beginning to sulk.

'What happened to D'Aramon?' Inji asked. 'Did he ever pick up your trail?'

Mama Rat shook her head. 'The reign of Louis Philippe ended a few years later. D'Aramon the spymaster lost his job. Even so, I didn't dare return to France. I wouldn't even now. There may still be people of his looking for me.'

'I never realised your life had been so ... interesting.' Sheba smiled. 'But, if the map was hidden, how did these people find out about it? And how did they connect it to Sister Moon?'

Mama Rat shook her head. 'I can only guess,' she said, 'they must have captured D'Aramon, or spoken to him somehow. Nobody but him and I knew it even existed. As for how they linked it to poor Moon ... I'm afraid I have no clue. Remy, dear, I must apologise for getting you and your mother involved in all this.'

'Mrs Rat,' said Remy. 'Please. Could you tell me where the map is? I don't want to make trouble for you, but my mother ...'

'Of course.' Mama Rat took a leather-bound notebook and a pencil from her coat pocket. She flipped it open and drew a symbol that looked like a letter 'm' with a barb on the tail, then tore out the page and handed it to Remy.

'Beneath the streets of Paris, there are catacombs,' she said. 'I'm sure you have heard of them.'

Remy nodded. His mother had told him about the underground maze that had been filled with skeletons when they emptied out the ancient cemeteries of the city. She'd told him how the walls had been lined with patterns made of skulls. How there were tunnels stacked to the roof with mountains of bone. She'd even suggested a rare trip outside of their apartment to visit it, but he had refused. All that death, those cramped tunnels underground. The thought had terrified him.

'In the ossuary, where the bones are stacked,' Mama Rat explained, 'there is a circular room called the Samaritan's Fountain. If you can find a skull in the wall with this symbol on, the map is rolled up and hidden inside.'

'Blimey,' said Pyewacket. 'Do you think you could have found somewhere creepier to hide it? I'm going to have nightmares just thinking about it.'

'How many skulls are in this wall?' Inji asked, staring at the mark on the paper.

'A lot,' said Remy. 'A very big lot.' He remembered reading about them in one of his history books. Ink etchings of layers upon layers of skulls, their empty eyes staring out at him.

Finding the map would not be easy. But at least it was a start. He had a chance, however slight, of setting his mother free. For her, he would gladly brave the creepy catacombs.

'Thank you,' he said to Mama Rat. She gave him a sad smile.

'One more thing,' said Sheba, as Mama Rat picked up her pipe and began to empty the bowl into an ashtray on the table. 'Do you still have any contacts in Paris? Anyone we could seek help from? When we go there, we will need allies and information. We must find these villains somehow, so we can trade the map for Sister Moon. We won't have any of the networks we have made here. No Gutter Brigade. No Inspector Abernathy.'

Mama Rat rubbed her chin. 'Well, dearie, it's many years since I was last there. And anyone that knew me now thinks I am dead. But there was one place ... a place where people like us performed in a show. Gigantus and I hid there for a bit, before we managed to escape to London. The owner was a brute, but there were many kind folk among the acts. If is still stands, the Théâtre de Rêves is the place you want to go.'

Remy drew a sharp breath. 'That's where my parents met!'

'Small world,' said Sheba. 'Although there can't be many such places in Paris. Do you know if it still exists, Remy?'

'I think so,' he said. 'Although Mother hardly speaks about it . . .'

'Well,' said Sheba. 'At least we know of one place we may be welcome. Thank you so much for your help, Mama.'

'I hope it does some good,' Mama Rat said. 'I really do. And I'm sorry Sister Moon had to suffer because of me. I wish I had never made that old lady tell her secret . . .'

'But then you would not have come to London, and we'd probably all still be working for that hideous Plumpscuttle,' said Sheba. She stood up and gave Mama a kiss on her cheek. 'We'll rescue Moon, don't worry. In fact, we had better return home straight away and begin to plan.'

'We should get back too,' said Gigantus. 'The Marquess will be wondering where we are ...'

With a chorus of goodbyes, handshakes and hugs, they all bundled out of the coffee shop. Mama Rat and Gigantus made their way back to the empty house on Walbrook, while the Carnival went to hail a carriage for the ride back across the river.

Perhaps, at any other time, Remy might have wondered more about Marie and her life with the mysterious Marquess of the Scarlequins, but all he could think about was counting the minutes until he was back in Paris, on the trail of this dangerous map.

CHAPTER SIX

*In which Remy discovers that
Sheba's everyday objects are
mostly deadly weapons.*

All the way home, through the throngs of traffic, the carriage was filled with chatter as the Carnival made plans. Talk of routes, booking passages, boats and trains ... it was enough to make Remy's head spin. Travelling officially seemed so much more complicated than sneaking on to a wagon or stowing away in a ship's hold.

He noticed Sil was back at his window, staring at the dark streets outside. His mouth was moving, as if he was silently talking to himself. Remy realised that Sil was the only Carnival member he hadn't spoken with yet. In fact, he realised, he hadn't even heard his voice. Perhaps he didn't like talking, or wasn't able to. But to just ignore him all the time seemed rude. Maybe he was scared and lonely, as Remy had been on his long journey from Paris to Calais.

'Excuse me,' Remy leaned close and whispered to him. 'What are you doing?'

Sil gave him a sidelong glance. Remy noticed his eyes – beneath that brow of heavy, knobbled bone – were a hazel colour, just like his sister Inji's (although, of course, without the cat-like slitted pupils).

For a second, he pressed his face closer to the window, as if he wanted to pretend Remy wasn't there. But then he spoke; his voice gentle and ghostly. 'I like to count the horses.'

'Can I count them too?' Remy asked. It seemed like the perfect way to take his mind off everything, even if it was just for a few moments. Sil moved his heavy head in what might have been a nod and Remy knelt at the window beside him, whispering numbers under his breath.

They were just rounding the corner into Paradise Street when Remy caught sight of a figure, standing beneath a lamp post. He froze, the blood turning to ice in his veins. Had there been a gleam of metal on the man's cheek? Had one of his eyes glowed with a dim, mechanical light?

He looked again, but the person had moved out of the circle of light. Shuffling, teetering from side to side along the pavement. Probably a drunk, staggering home from a night in a gin palace and not Thom at all.

Probably.

*

'Two hundred and fifty-six,' Sil whispered, just as they pulled up at the Carnival's house.

'Me too,' Remy said, forcing himself to smile even though his stomach was still clenched in fright.

As Pyewacket opened the carriage door and they all began to climb out, Inji hung back to speak to him.

'That was very kind, the way you spoke to Sil,' she said. 'He must really like you – it normally takes him months to trust strangers.'

'Is he scared of them?' Remy asked. He felt that

way about new people himself, although he was mostly frightened about how they were going to react at the sight of him.

'Not really,' she said. 'He just feels things differently to us. He doesn't like loud noises or the way certain things feel. And if there's any change from what he's used to, he gets upset.'

Remy thought about his life in the Montmartre apartment. How every day was exactly the same, and how terrifying it had been when it all got turned upside down. 'I can understand that,' he said.

Inji gave him another smile, and then sprang out of the carriage, landing silently on the cobbles outside, leaving Remy to follow, back into the house.

*

When he walked into the front parlour, he found a new person standing there. A young man, fashionably dressed in a smart, grey-checked suit, the coat of which reached almost to his knees. He had a mass of thick black hair, tightly curled, which had been scraped back into a ponytail. A neat pair of sideburns, immaculately trimmed, ran down to his jawline, and his waistcoat sported a gleaming watch chain. His outfit was finished off with a silk cravat covered in gold and silver numbers, and a matching pocket square. He was smiling and nodding at the rest of the Carnival as if he knew them well. Sil even walked up to him and held out one of his chunky, bone-covered hands to be squeezed.

'Remy,' said Sheba. 'This is Glyph. I mentioned him to you earlier.'

'Oh yes,' said Remy. *The magician who helps solve crimes*, he remembered. *And whose old clothes I'm wearing.* 'Hello. Thank you for the suit.'

Glyph nodded his head and waved. Remy noticed he had kind eyes; deep brown, with dark lashes.

'He doesn't speak,' said Pyewacket. 'In case you think he's being rude. He's got an amazing Gift, though. Here, write down a number. Make it as big as you like.'

He handed Remy a sheet of paper and a pencil from a side table. Sheba tutted (something she seemed to do a lot around Pyewacket). 'Really, we haven't got time for parlour tricks.'

'No, this is great,' said Pyewacket. 'Go on!' He

stared at Remy with those goggling yellow eyes until he started to write. *878*, he scribbled, and then handed the paper back.

'Is that all? You could have gone up to eight digits, at least! Never mind. Watch this – go on, Glyphster. Do your stuff!'

With a sigh, Glyph reached into the pocket of his smart jacket and brought out a set of playing cards. The backs were patterned, like a usual deck, but the fronts had large letters and numbers printed on them instead of Jacks, Queens and suits. With long, quick fingers Glyph flipped, shuffled and riffled them and then snapped three down on the walnut coffee table in the centre of the room. *Fnap, fnap, fnap!*

Remy edged over to look, and was amazed to see the same numbers he had written: 8-7-8.

'Is it a magic trick?' he asked. His mother had told him about conjurors and illusionists at the theatre where she had worked. They made things disappear, or change shape or burst into flocks of doves. But, she had said, none of it was real.

'It's just what he does,' Inji explained. 'And also, how he used to speak. Although now he's learnt a bit of sign language too.'

'Glyph,' said Sheba. 'Did you find anything out about this *L'Araignée*? This Spider?'

Glyph nodded, and reached for a manila folder he had placed on one of the chairs. It was stuffed full of paperwork, which Sheba began to flick through. Her amber eyes zipped across the pages – surely she couldn't be reading that quickly?

'Hmm,' she said, after only a few moments. 'It appears that the Spider and her gang have been under the eye of Glyph's friends at Scotland Yard. Not only have they been operating in France, but here in Britain, as well.'

'Do they know who they are?' asked Remy. 'Have they kidnapped anyone else?'

'It doesn't say.' Sheba flipped a few more pages. 'They have just recently been noticed. Nobody knows their identity, only that they have taken over several smuggling operations, bringing in illegal items from across the Channel.'

'Could they have been here twenty years ago?' Pyewacket asked. 'That's when Sister Moon and Mama Rat lived together. It might be how the Spider knows they are connected.'

'Maybe they even come from London,' Inji

suggested. 'If it was twenty years ago, they could have been quite young. Perhaps they visited the Carnival when it was Plumpscuttle's sideshow?'

Sheba nodded. 'Perhaps. We must assume they saw or heard of the show back then – Mama and Moon haven't been anywhere near each other since. But there were hundreds of people tramping through that house on Brick Lane every week. Without more to go on, this Spider could be anybody.'

As Sheba continued to flip through the file, Glyph reached over and pointed to a passage on the last page.

'It says here,' said Sheba, 'that, although the Spider's identity is unknown, they do have a description of a suspect. A man whose face was half covered with a metal plate.'

'I know that man!' Remy's shout made everyone jump. 'He was one of the gang that took me and my mother! He had a steel mask, with a hinge that let him move his jaw. But he can't be the Spider . . . he always talked as if the Spider was his boss.'

'Did you ever hear his name mentioned?' Sheba asked. 'Were there any clues as to who he might be?'

Remy nodded. He had heard their captors talking

to each other, using names from an old nursery rhyme. They had even laughed at how clever they were.

'They called him Thom,' he said. '*Thom le poucet.*'

'Tom Thumb. But perhaps he might actually be a Thomas. One who might have had an accident that injured his face. Not much to go on, but it's a start.' Sheba handed the file back to Glyph, who touched a finger to his ears, then eyes. *I'll keep looking into it.*

'Now,' said Sheba. 'I know it's getting late, but I think we should begin packing. I'd like to set off for Paris as soon as tickets can be arranged.'

Glyph cleared his throat and took his cards from his pocket again. In a flurry of snaps, he laid a series of them out on the table. L-N-S-U-R-R-E-N-D-E-R read the first row. A-R-M-Y-B-E-A-T-E-N.

'Dickens's dipstick!' Pyewacket said. 'L.N. Is Louis Napoleon, the French emperor! He's surrendered to the Prussians!'

'This does complicate things,' said Sheba. 'Is the war between France and Prussia over, then?'

Glyph shook his head. He gathered up his cards, sent them fluttering from hand to hand in the air, then snapped some more down in a line. M-A-R-C-H-I-N-G-O-N-P-A-R-I-S.

'The Prussian army is marching on Paris?' Pyewacket's face went pale beneath his whiskers. 'But that's where we're going! We'll be trapped in a war zone!'

'Calm down,' said Inji. 'France is pretty big, isn't it? How long will it take them to get there, do you think?'

Glyph shrugged and held up two fingers. His other hand gave a see-saw motion.

'Possibly two weeks?' Sheba said. 'That should give us plenty of time. And, if we do get stuck, I'm sure we'll cope. I intend on taking some serious supplies.'

'What kind?' Remy asked, imagining them hauling crates of food and lemonade through the Parisian streets. The strange looks they would get, and then the even stranger ones when the citizens saw who was doing the hauling.

'Ah.' Sheba smiled at him. 'There's a room in the house I think you should see.'

*

Leaving the others to discuss arrangements, Sheba led Remy out of the parlour and along the corridor to the kitchen. About halfway down, she stopped and pressed against a section of the wood-panelled wall. A muffled *click* sounded, and a hidden doorway swung open.

'Secret workshop,' said Sheba, with a wink, and then disappeared inside.

Remy followed, discovering a steep stone staircase that led down into the shadows. He felt the darkness calling to him; could smell its chill dampness. There were different kinds of dark, he had discovered. The cool dusk of a summer night, the quiet murk of old, empty buildings. Down there was the deep dankness of loamy soil, moist from thousands of years of river water passing nearby. He headed down the steps, breathing it in ... and then Sheba lit a gas lamp on the wall, filling the place with light.

Reeling from the sudden loss of soothing dark, Remy tottered down the last few steps and found himself in an old stone cellar that had been transformed into a modern workshop. There were two long workbenches against the walls, stacked with machinery and mechanical parts. A drawing board covered with blueprints stood in the corner, and the whitewashed bricks around it were plastered with sketches and diagrams of inventions. There was also a smaller bench, this one holding a cluster of glass bottles, tubes, pipes and beakers. A round jar of purple liquid was bubbling away above a hissing Bunsen burner.

'Are you ... a scientist?' Remy stared around the room in awe. He couldn't take his eyes off all the incredible devices. He was especially fascinated by the cooking chemicals.

'Not really,' says Sheba. 'I have a passion for inventing things. I've created many little odds and ends that help us in our work.'

'What are you making here?' Remy asked. He had walked over to the bubbling apparatus, watching the smoke as it evaporated from the beaker and condensed into clear droplets along a long, glass tube before trickling down into another jar.

'Ah.' Sheba walked over and examined the beaker, turning down the gas flow on the burner slightly. 'I am trying to create an anaesthetic ... a mixture that will make someone fall asleep for a period of time and feel no pain.'

'Is it to knock out villains?' Remy asked, hopeful. If they could make those metal monsters unconscious, then they could just untie his mother and escape. No fighting necessary.

'I'm afraid not,' said Sheba. 'It's for Sil. You may have noticed that he has trouble breathing and moving because of the bone plates on his body?'

Remy nodded. When he was kneeling next to him in the carriage, he could hear the constant wheezing as he fought for breath.

'He wasn't always like that. The plates keep growing and thickening as he gets older. I'm afraid there's nothing we can do, except perhaps cut them back. But to perform surgery like that, he would have to be made to sleep for a very long time. Hours, maybe. We could use ether or chloroform, but they just aren't good enough.'

'What ... what will happen if you don't help him?' Remy had a horrid feeling he didn't want to hear the answer.

'He will find it harder and harder to breathe,' Sheba said, sadly. 'And eventually ...'

'You *will* be able to do something, though, won't you?' Remy had only briefly spoken to Sil, but it was enough to have formed a bond. The thought of him suffocating within his own body . . .

'I'm sure I will,' said Sheba. 'And we have the best surgeons in London working on his case. I have high hopes.'

Remy relaxed a little. He watched the frothing liquid some more, wondering at how a certain mixture of the right ingredients could be made to do whatever you wanted. It was a kind of magic, he supposed. Like witches mixing potions in cauldrons.

'Do you think,' he said, 'that a mixture could be made to help my skin? To stop it burning in the sun?'

Sheba looked at him for a moment, staring intensely at his cheeks, his forehead. Remy could almost see the seed of the idea he had just planted start to grow. 'You know, perhaps it could,' she said. 'Would you like to try out some ideas with me? After we have rescued your mother?'

At those very words, Remy felt a door opening in his head. Just a crack, at first, but on the other side were all the things he had ever dreamed of: walking through the Tuileries gardens in the sunshine; sitting on a hill outside Paris, picnicking under a blue sky;

running along a beach somewhere, jumping in and out of the waves.

'Yes, please,' he said. 'I would like that *very* much.'

'Excellent,' said Sheba, clapping her hands. 'It will be lovely to have a pupil. Inji has never been interested in science, Glyph just wants to perform magic tricks and Sil ... well, he has his own particular fascinations. And I won't even mention the times I've tried to teach Pyewacket *anything*. But in the meantime – we have some packing to do.'

Remy watched as Sheba pulled a travelling trunk out from under one of the benches and began to fill it with items from the shelves. Make-up cases, fountain pens, hairpins, perfume bottles, a parasol ... it looked as though she was preparing for a luxurious holiday rather than a rescue mission.

'Um,' he said, wondering how to put it politely. 'Shouldn't you be bringing some equipment? Something to defend ourselves with, maybe?'

'Ah,' said Sheba, winking at him. 'I am.' She began to hold up the things in the trunk. 'This pen holds a set of lock picks. This snuff container is really a smoke grenade. My antique brooch has a roll of wire inside – strong enough to hold an adult's weight. These hairpins are syringes, for injecting enemies with tranquillisers. And my lace parasol is actually a rifle.'

'*Oh, la vache!*' Remy said, shocked into speaking French for a moment. 'What else do you have?'

'Lots,' said Sheba. She went to one of the benches and began opening drawers. 'For Inji: a waistcoat lined with several layers of fine steel mesh. Knife-proof and will – hopefully – stop a bullet. For Pyewacket: a pair of brass-rimmed goggles that will help him see in the dark. And by adjusting this dial, he can increase the magnification and look at things much further away.'

'And what's that?' Remy asked, pointing at a small pistol with a wooden handle and a clockwork key on the side.

'This?' Sheba held it up, turning it so Remy could see the little revolving chamber and the tiny barrel. 'My clockwork gun. I found this on our first ever job, nearly twenty years ago. I always take it with me now. It brings me luck.'

As Sheba laid these items carefully in the trunk, Remy wondered about the other Carnival members.

'What about Sil and Glyph? Did you make things for them?'

Sheba shook her head, sadly. 'Sil won't be coming, I'm afraid. He doesn't cope very well with sudden changes, and heading into Paris during a war … well, it would probably cause him great distress. Glyph will stay here to look after him, and also to provide us with any support we might need, if we have problems.'

'Oh,' said Remy. 'I see.' He would have liked all his new friends beside him, but he didn't want to see Sil upset.

'I do have one more thing, though,' said Sheba. 'A very special surprise.'

From the drawer, she drew out a lacquered box. Opening the lid, she revealed two large hunting knives, with blades almost as long as Remy's forearms. Their metal was covered with fine ripples of light and dark steel, tapering down to gleaming edges that whispered sharpness. They were beautiful, but deadly; like the curve of a shark's fin cutting through water or the flicker of a snake's scales in the long grass.

'Mother had some like that,' Remy whispered.

'I know,' said Sheba. 'I had these made for her, many years ago, when I thought she might one day come back to London. I used a blacksmith who knew how to fold steel hundreds of times, making it incredibly strong. The handles are wrapped in shark skin, for better grip. We will give them to her, once we've found her. Do you think she'll like them?'

Remy imagined his mother wielding one in each hand, ebony eyes sparkling, black hair flowing as she closed in on the thugs who had captured her.

'Oh, yes,' he said. 'I expect she will like them a *lot.*'

CHAPTER SEVEN

*In which the Carnival
go on a train journey.*

At some point, among all the hefting of luggage trunks and folding of clothes, Remy had been given a mug of cocoa and sent up to bed. Exhausted again, he fell asleep before he even had time to undress, and was woken at dawn by an excited Pyewacket drawing his bedroom curtains.

'Please don't!' Remy shouted, as square patches of deadly sunlight streaked across the room. He pulled the covers over his head, hiding from them.

'Oh, cripes! Forgot about that!' Pyewacket quickly shut the curtains again. 'Sorry, old bean! It's time to get up, though. We're on the seven o'clock train to Dover.'

'Dover?' Remy struggled out of the bedclothes and yawned. He felt like he still needed another ten hours' sleep.

'For the steamer to Calais,' Pyewacket explained. 'We'll not be hiding in the hold of a merchant ship from the docks, like the one you came across on. First-class transport all the way, thanks to Sheba. And you might want to think about changing out of those clothes. You look like an elephant sat on you.'

Remy looked down at the crumpled velvet jacket and trousers he had slept in. He was about to protest that he didn't have anything else to wear, when he noticed another suit laid out on a chair. This one was a rich plum colour, and had a matching peaked cap.

'See you downstairs for breakfast in ten minutes,' said Pyewacket, with a wave. And he loped out of the bedroom on his knuckles.

*

Once he was dressed in his new plum suit – with Pamplemousse safely stowed in his jacket pocket – Remy made his way downstairs. A buzz of voices came from the kitchen at the back of the house. Walking down the corridor, he passed a small stack of trunks and suitcases in the hallway and wondered how many of them were filled with actual clothes and how much was, instead, weapons in disguise.

Inside the kitchen, everyone was sitting around a large table heaped with slices of toast, mounds of fried eggs, rashers of fried bacon, dishes of devilled kidneys and several pots of Crosse and Blackwell's anchovy paste (for sandwiches, &c).

'Grab a seat!' Pyewacket yelled, and poured him a cup of steaming coffee. Inji gave him a plate, and shovelled it high with a bit of everything.

'I don't think I can eat all that,' Remy said, feeling his skin turn even more green than usual.

'Nonsense!' Pyewacket spoke through a mouthful of sausage. 'It'll put hairs on your knuckles!'

'That's only in your case,' said Inji, looking at him over the rim of her coffee cup.

'Just eat what you can,' said Sheba. 'I know there's an absolute tonne. But we all grew up eating scraps of gruel or fried mutton – if we were lucky – so we have a lot of breakfasting to make up for!'

Remy nibbled a slice of toast, wishing there were some croissants instead. He noticed everyone was dressed in practical travelling clothes: in muted colours, with lots of pockets everywhere. He could feel a flutter of nerves begin to unfold in his belly. More than anything, he wanted to see his mother again. But travelling back towards Paris – every step would take him closer to danger. He would have to see those mechanical monsters again. Maybe even their boss, this Spider. What if they were even worse?

'Remy,' said Sheba, putting a stop to his worrying. 'Before we leave, I have something to show you.'

Draped over the back of her chair was a piece of black material. She stood and shook it out, revealing a cloth mask with lenses of smoked glass covering the eyes. As Remy frowned, she walked over and began to fit it over his head.

'I was up most of the night making this,' she explained. 'I've used three layers of material. It should be enough to block out the sun's rays. And with gloves to cover your hands, you should be safe to move around in daylight.'

The mask was hot, and made it difficult to

breathe. The glass lenses steamed up a little, and looking through them was like peering out of a muddy fishbowl, but to be able to go outside in the sunshine ... it wasn't quite his dream of feeling the sun on his skin, the waves at his feet. But it was several steps closer than he had ever been.

'Thank you,' he said, his voice muffled. Pyewacket balanced the plum velvet cap on top of Remy's head.

'There,' he said, grinning. 'Now you look as strange as the rest of us.'

*

Waterloo train station was easily the biggest and noisiest building Remy had ever been in. He had seen the Gare du Nord in Paris from a distance – its glass and steel roof shouldering its way up among the houses around it – but had never ventured inside. He was sure it couldn't be as loud and packed as this place was, though. It was like stepping into the middle of six thunderstorms, all raging at once.

They were walking along a line of ten or more platforms, most of them hosting a chuffing, hooting, clanking iron beast. Steam trains. At least eight of them stood, like resting dragons, their long bodies being slowly filled with streams of passengers. The air was thick with the smell of burning coal and hot oil. Ladies with enormous skirts bumped and jostled him from all sides, and he peered out from his glass goggles at it all – casting many nervous glances up at the sunlight that lanced down through the panes of glass in the station roof, praying that Sheba's mask would stop his skin from burning. His ears, deafened by the station noise and muffled by the thick fabric mask, still strained to hear any trace of that ominous *ticktickticking*. Somehow, he couldn't shake the feeling that one of those monsters was close by; had always been within a few steps of him. That man in the greatcoat by the newspaper stand – had there been a gleam of steel as he turned his head? What about that fellow carrying the bale of cloth on his shoulder – was it to disguise the side of his face? Had that glaring blue eye been the same as Thom's?

But it was impossible to see clearly in all this bustle. Louis Napoleon himself could have just brushed shoulders with him, and he wouldn't have noticed.

Up ahead, Pyewacket and Inji were pushing luggage trolleys, stacked high with their trunks and bags. Remy gripped Pamplemousse in one gloved hand, the other holding tight to Sheba as she followed in their wake. She held a bunch of tickets, and was checking the numbers of the platforms.

'Number three,' she called, her voice lost in the hubbub of shouting as hundreds of people all tried to make their voices heard above the engines. 'The one with the red train.'

They began to manoeuvre their way towards their platform. Every now and then a gaggle of gentlemen barged past on their way to work, their canes swinging, newspapers gripped under their arms. The station was lined with stalls and barrows selling hot pies, bottles of lemonade and twists of roasted chestnuts. People marched in all directions, all with such purpose and speed. It seemed so very ... *modern*.

Sheba stopped by a guard in a waistcoat and shiny peaked cap. 'Excuse me,' she said. 'Is this the train for Dover?'

'Seven o'clock to Dover, ma'am,' said the guard, flipping open the cover of his silver watch to check the time. 'Best be quick. She leaves in three minutes.'

He popped his watch into a pocket, then touched the peak of his cap in politeness. He looked like he might have been about to offer some help, but his gaze fell on Inji with her man's clothes and cat's eyes. Then on Pyewacket, with his dangling arms and jutting tusks. Finally, he spotted Remy, covered head to foot in cloth, like a living toy doll, one hand of which clutched a smashed-up Pierrot head, its single goggling eye staring upwards.

They left him gaping, dumbstruck, his mouth slowly opening and closing.

*

'All aboard,' said Pyewacket, as he set his luggage cart down beside a first-class carriage. Inji opened the door and sprang in, then began stowing the trunks away on shelves that jutted out over the seats.

Remy stood and stared at the train's engine. Their carriage was right behind it, and he could see the fireman shovelling coal from a towering mound into the fiery mouth of the boiler. The driver stood beside him, checking the gauges as the train built up steam.

'Wonderful piece of engineering, isn't it?' Sheba said to him, half shouting over the noise. 'Have you ever ridden on a train before?'

Remy shook his head. The rhythmic *chuff-chuff-chuff* reminded him of the paddle steamer he had been hiding in, just yesterday morning.

'They are smooth and quick as anything these days,' said Sheba. 'They can even go as fast as thirty miles an hour! We'll be in Dover by the afternoon.'

Drawing him away from the platform, Sheba helped Remy up the step and into the carriage. It was like a small room, with two sets of crimson upholstered seats facing each other. A wood-panelled wall with large windows and a door faced them. On the other side was a corridor that ran the length of the train, and then another set of windows beyond.

Pyewacket was already seated, leaning back and munching on a piece of black pudding he had saved from breakfast. Other travellers were passing up and down the corridor outside, peering in to see if there were any spare seats. Inji reached up and pulled the blinds down, before sitting herself. She looked at Remy and patted the seat next to her.

When he and Sheba had taken their places, a guard walked down the platform outside, slamming the train doors to make sure they were shut. The sudden bang made Remy jump. Then a whistle blew, the engine let out a dragon's breath of steam, and they began to pull out of the station.

*

They moved slowly at first, edging their way along the rails, past the long lines of the other trains, then through a landscape of endless tracks, railway sheds and buildings that all seemed to be covered in a thick layer of black grime.

Once the wide fan of tracks had narrowed, they began to pick up speed, chuffing their way past rows of houses and factories with spindly chimneys. The train clunked out a steady rhythm as it rolled along the track, matching the endless *chuff-chuff-chuff* of the steam. The carriage rocked from side to side, making the springs in the seat squeak. It was like listening to a piece of music, composed for a very strange set of instruments.

And then, in a blink, they had left London. The sooty brickwork and sea of clustered roofs suddenly vanished. Trees appeared, and hedges. Houses with gardens. Parks. Duck ponds. A few moments later, and they were among rolling fields, with only the odd farmhouse to break up the view. Animals grazed – creatures Remy had hardly seen from his life in his Paris apartment. Sheep, cows, geese, pigs ... he recognised them from picture books. And everything around was so *green*.

He held up Pamplemousse to see, marvelling at the thick trees as they passed through a wood. The way the light fell in overlapping patches of colour. The soft, flowing shapes of everything ... for someone used to seeing only the solid, hard-edged blocks of buildings, it was like a new, alien world.

'Your doll has seen better days, hasn't it?' Pyewacket said, staring at Pamplemousse. 'Did you find it on a dump or something?'

'He's very old,' Remy muttered, tucking him back into his jacket pocket. 'He's been dropped a lot of times.'

'Didn't you ever have a tatty plaything, when you were poor?' Inji glared at Pyewacket. 'I made myself a doll out of twigs and rags, when I was in the workhouse. Carried it everywhere.'

'Were things really that bad for you and Sister Moon? Is that the only plaything you could afford?' Sheba asked. Her voice had a catch in it, as if she was about to cry.

'No,' said Remy, quickly. 'We had money from Mother's work. She bought me lots of toys: wooden blocks, a miniature circus. And books too – in French, English and Mandarin. Pamplemousse is broken because I've had him so long. I've always slept with him at night. He's ... he's like a friend.'

'He must be very special,' Inji said, with a smile.

'He is,' said Remy. 'My father gave him to me. Before he died. It's the only thing I have to remember him by.'

Pyewacket made a strangled sound and hid his face in his hands. 'Sorry, Remy,' he spoke through his hairy fingers. 'I didn't mean to be rude. These things just come out. I can't help it.'

'It's fine,' said Remy. And he eased Pamplemousse out of his pocket so he could give Pyewacket a nod.

Among the stack of trunks was a wicker picnic hamper. They hadn't gone far when Pyewacket heaved it down from the luggage and opened the lid.

'Time for elevenses,' he said, licking his lips. He began to remove pots, bottles and covered plates, placing them on the seats. Remy spotted a jug of ginger beer, half a roast chicken, gammon sandwiches, pigeon pies and a slab of tongue.

'My breakfast has hardly gone down,' said Sheba, shaking her head. 'That food is supposed to last us until supper time!'

'Oh, Queen Vic's dirty bloomers!' Pyewacket cursed. 'I've gone and forgotten the cake! It was an apple turnover as well. I must have left it on the kitchen table. I bet Sil's eaten it already.'

'I really think we'll be fine with what we have,' said Inji. 'How are you going to climb the Paris rooftops when your pot-belly is the size of a baby hippo?'

'My belly is perfectly flat, thank you,' said Pyewacket, sucking in his tummy. 'I shall have to go and buy cake from the restaurant car. Do you fancy coming, Remy?'

He was smiling kindly, perhaps hoping to make up for his earlier comment about Pamplemousse. But Remy didn't feel confident enough to leave the carriage. Not when he was still covered up in his sun-proof mask.

As if reading his mind, Sheba mimed taking the thing off. 'I think you might be able to go without it on the train,' she said. 'There's plenty of shadows about. You should be able to keep out of the sunlight.'

With relief, Remy peeled off the mask and breathed in a lungful of air. It was so hot under there: his hair was slicked with sweat and his cheeks like little beetroots. Sure enough, the daylight inside the compartment wasn't strong enough to affect him. Even so, he still felt nervous about walking into a dining car full of people.

'Are you coming, then?' Pyewacket asked, beginning to open the door.

'I . . . I don't . . .' Remy tried to explain. Instead he just pointed at his face. At his deep crimson eyes and pale green skin. At the pinpricks of fangs on his lip and the tips of his elfin ears.

'Pah!' Pyewacket pointed at his own features. 'Don't be worried about what people think of you.

I've had stares and laughs and mean comments my whole life. But they can say what they like about how you look – they don't know anything about *you*. Not the real you. And that's the only part that matters.'

'He's right, Remy,' said Inji. 'Hold your head high. We all think you're amazing. Who cares what rude, stupid strangers might say?'

Remy cringed. Just the thought of walking past other passengers in broad daylight made his legs feel weak. But he was supposed to be on a rescue mission. How would he be able to save his mother if he couldn't even walk along a train? 'All right, then. I'll go,' he said, taking a deep breath. He clutched Pamplemousse almost hard enough to crack him into pieces again.

'Brilliant,' said Pyewacket. 'Let's go and find some cake.'

*

They stepped into the corridor, and started walking down the narrow passage. On Remy's left, fields and trees whipped past the windows. On his right there were more compartments, each one filled with passengers who were chatting, reading books or nodding off to sleep.

The train rocked as it moved, making it hard to walk. Remy swayed to and fro, reaching out to grab Pyewacket every now and then as they went over a bump in the line.

At the end of the carriage they had to open another door and then step over the gap into the next wagon. Below him, Remy could see the link where the two carriages were joined. It shook and rattled, as if it might break free at any minute and he could see a blur of the track, whipping by underneath. And, as if that weren't bad enough, above him was the sky and the glaring sun. He felt it begin to heat his face, even in the split second before he jumped across.

Pyewacket was already over, holding open the door to the restaurant car for him. 'I hate that bit,' he said. 'Always think I'll slip and go tumbling under the train.'

Remy swallowed hard and nodded, wishing he had stayed back in the safe, cosy compartment with the others. *Be brave*, he told himself. *If you can sneak your way from Paris to London, you can do this as well.*

The restaurant car had tables on either side, and was filled with smartly dressed gentlefolk, sipping tea and eating their breakfast. The men had placed their top hats on the seats next to them, the women wore teetering bonnets with feathers and ribbon sticking out everywhere. There was a quiet hum of conversation, and a constant tinkling as the light fittings on the ceiling were jiggled by the train's movement.

A waiter was making his way up the centre aisle towards them, balancing several teapots on a tray and somehow managing not to spill them, even as he swayed from side to side.

'Excuse me, my good man,' said Pyewacket, in his posh gentleman's voice. 'I was wondering if it would be possible to purchase some form of cake. I appear to have misplaced my apple turnover, don't you know.'

The waiter looked down at the odd pair standing in front of him in stunned silence. Remy could actually see the blood drain from his face.

'I . . . uh . . .' he stuttered.

'Cake?' Pyewacket reminded him.

'The dining car is for *first-class* passengers only,' the waiter managed to say.

'We *are* first class,' Pyewacket said, still smiling. 'I can show you our tickets, if you like. Now. About that cake?'

'We ... we don't serve the likes of you,' said the waiter. 'You'll have to leave.'

'The likes of us?' Pyewacket's smile became a snarl. 'How dare you? We paid for our tickets, just like everyone else in here. You're saying you won't serve us, just because of how we look?'

Heads all around the carriage were turning to stare. Remy tugged on Pye's jacket. 'Can we just go? *Please?*'

Pyewacket seemed to notice the eyes on them, the muttering voices. He must know there was going to be a scene if he carried on. Remy tugged at his coat again, and pleaded with his eyes.

'Come, Remy,' Pyewacket said, finally, his nose in the air. 'We shall see if there is a place to buy cake further down the train. It smells funny in here anyway.'

With his chin jutting and chest puffed out, he began to walk down the aisle, letting all the whispered comments fizzle out in his wake. Wishing he could be so bold, Remy scuttled along behind. He couldn't help but hear some of the things the diners said.

'What on earth are they?'

'Have they escaped from a circus?'

'. . . put me right off me kippers!'

He was relieved when they reached the end of the carriage and stepped through the door, although he could still hear muffled exclamations of surprise from behind him. If anything, they were even growing louder.

'Sorry about that,' Pyewacket said. 'Might have known it would happen.'

'Does it always?' Remy asked, once they had made the terrifying step between the cars again. He was used to hiding away from people. If he had to face unkindness like that every time he showed himself, keeping out of sight seemed the best option.

'Most of the time,' said Pyewacket, with a sigh. 'The best you can hope for is that they just stare. You get used to it, I suppose. Except you don't. Not really.'

Remy decided it was better to change the subject. 'What's in this part of the train?' he asked, peering through the door window in front of them.

'Blowed if I know,' said Pyewacket. 'Second and third class, I expect. I bet they're not as stuffy as that lot of toffs. Silver spoons in their mouths, the lot of them.'

Remy hadn't noticed the cutlery they were using. He was sure some of it had been forks. Perhaps Pyewacket was confused in his anger – or maybe it was another English expression.

Opening the door to the next carriage, they found themselves in a long, windowless wagon. The walls and floor were bare wooden planks, and the only contents were hundreds of large sacks, stacked in piles.

'Must be the mail coach,' said Pyewacket. 'No cake in here. Let's keep going.'

Remy really didn't feel like heading further down the train. Any courage he had was now long gone. It had disappeared when that waiter had been so horrible. Still, the only other choice was to turn back and he didn't feel like walking through the restaurant car again so soon after they had left.

He followed Pyewacket down the coach, past the heaps of brown sacks. All those letters . . . there must be thousands of them. The sacks jiggled along with the train's rhythm, adding their rustling to the sound of the rails. *Clackety-clack, clackety-clack.* And also *tickticktickticktickticktick* . . .

Remy froze.

That sound again. That ticking clockwork, hidden beneath all the other layers of noise.

Holding his breath, Remy turned around, hoping against hope that his imagination was playing tricks on him.

It wasn't.

There, standing in the doorway they had just stepped through, was one of the Spider's henchmen. The one they called Thom. The man with the metal face. It was true. He had been following Remy the whole time, ever since he left Paris, waiting to see if he found Sheba, waiting to try and snatch the map . . .

There was a slight squeal as the man's iron jaw opened, just wide enough to let out a little chuckle.

Chapter Eight

*In which Remy finds trains can
be unexpectedly dangerous.*

Thom took a step closer to Remy, balancing himself against the train movement. Remy could see the familiar hinged jaw that covered the side of his chin; cogs and gears peeking out, underneath the plating. They slowly ground together, making that ticking sound. A brown eye peered from a hole in the tiny panels of riveted steel running over his left cheek, matching the one on the fleshy part of his face. The human half of his mouth was twisted in a mean smile. One that promised this meeting was going to end very painfully.

By instinct, Remy reached out to the shadows,

trying to whip them around himself, to hide from this monster. But it didn't work – it was no good when they could already see you – and there was nowhere he could run. The mail car was just a long, thin trap.

'Are you coming, Remy?' Pyewacket called from behind him. Then, as he saw the hulking figure of Thom: 'What the . . .?'

'Run,' Remy tried to shout, but it just came out as a whisper. His throat had closed up. His legs had frozen in place. Cold fear crackled through his body, as it had on that first night, when they crashed into his apartment.

'I see you've found some friends,' Thom said, taking another step. There was a weapon clutched in his right hand. Some kind of stubby wooden stick. 'Have they given you the map?'

'N-no,' Remy whispered. He tried to edge his feet back, but they wouldn't move.

'I don't believe you,' Thom said, his eyes flashing with hate. 'Give it to me now, before I hurt you.'

'Oi, tin face!' Pyewacket stepped in front of Remy, shielding him from the villain. 'Why don't you pick on someone your own size?'

'My pleasure,' said Thom. He swung the club he was holding, catching Pyewacket across the side of his head, sending him crumpling to the floor as senseless as one of the stuffed sacks all around him.

Remy did run, then. He turned and started to sprint for the far end of the carriage, but Thom was too quick. Strong fingers gripped the back of Remy's collar and he felt himself being yanked off his feet. He flailed in mid-air for a moment, before he was slammed up against the wooden wall. All the air was knocked out of him in a painful whoosh.

'The map!' Thom shouted in his face. 'Give it to me now, and I won't have to hurt your friend!'

'The only person that's going to get hurt is *you*.' A voice came from behind Thom, packed with hiss and venom. Remy bent his head to look and there – like some kind of feline guardian angel – was Inji. She had padded in through the open carriage door without anyone noticing, following Thom even as he had been following them. Just like a train-based game of cat and mouse.

But she didn't look like the usual prowling, poised girl he was used to seeing. Her teeth were bared, sharp and gleaming. Her hair stood up in a

shock of spikes, and there was thick fur on her face, bristling in fury. She had taken off her gloves, and curved white claws lanced through the tips of her fingers, tapering to points so sharp, they were almost invisible.

In one quick movement, Thom dropped Remy and swept the arm that had been pinning him around in a blow that would have knocked Inji to the other end of the mail car. If, of course, she had still been there.

Too fast to even see, she ducked, bounced up and lashed out with a fistful of claws, ripping open four gashes in the arm of Thom's jacket as if it were made of tissue paper.

It all happened in a blink, before Remy had even hit the ground. By the time his bottom had connected with the floorboards, Inji was somewhere else, striking with her other hand. Thom roared and punched at her, missing again and again. Inji was too quick for him to even touch her.

Remy scuttled over to Pyewacket, who was still out cold. Not knowing what else to do, he grabbed one of his great, hairy hands and held tight, pulling the shadows about the pair of them as best he could.

He wasn't sure why he even did it – it was just his instinct to hide.

Meanwhile, Inji was still dodging, with Thom trying harder and harder to hit her. The man was screaming with rage now, his half-metal mouth clanging open and shut as he bellowed. His jacket had been reduced to a mass of tatters and there were red lines of scratches all over his face. He looked like he'd been rolling in a bramble patch.

Duck, slash, duck, slash … Inji never stopped moving, never stopped slicing with those claws. But her strikes weren't deadly, Remy realised. Just enough to keep her target stampeding, stepping forward with each attack. She was leading him back through the carriage, right up to the …

Her final leap made her crash up against the open door. There was nowhere left to jump to.

'Got you!' Thom shouted, lunging forward with both hands, ready to grip Inji by the throat. Remy almost shrieked – until he saw the smug look on Inji's face. The cat that got the cream. She had set the trap and Thom had stumbled straight into it.

One last time, she ducked under his arms, rolled along the floor behind him, and then bounced up again, just in time to place a kick right in the middle of his back. With a scream that rapidly vanished, Thom fell out of the carriage door, hit the back of the dining car, and then tumbled out of sight, down on to the tracks.

The train just continued running. *Clackety-clack, clackety-clack, clackety-clack.*

'Are you hurt?' Inji left the open doorway and rushed over to him. She seemed to spot him instantly, despite the darkness he had conjured. But then he noticed her cat's eyes gleaming. The shadows were her friend too.

'No,' he managed to say, although his throat felt bruised. And his whole body was shaking with fright. 'He hit Pyewacket, though . . .'

Inji bent down and felt the side of Pyewacket's head. He moaned and began to move, much to Remy's relief.

'One of them's here,' he mumbled. 'Metal-face. I deduce it's one of the blighters that snatched Moonie.'

'Well, of course he was,' said Inji, hauling the little man up to his feet. 'But you don't have to worry about him any more. He's decided to catch another train.'

Remy looked at the open door in horror, imagining what happened to Thom as he fell. 'Was he . . . did he . . . go under the wheels?' he asked.

Inji shrugged. 'I think he fell clear. Although I can't be sure. Either way, that's one less of them. Come on. Let's get back to the others, where we can keep a proper eye on you.'

'I didn't get cake!' Pyewacket began to protest, but Inji was already heaving him towards the door. Remy followed, as close as he could. Staying as near to Inji as possible seemed like the best idea he'd had in ages.

*

They arrived in Dover later that afternoon. The rest of the journey had been spent in their compartment, nursing Pyewacket's head, as he munched his way through the picnic hamper. His story of the battle with Thom had been retold several times, with his role in it becoming braver and more impressive with each version. He was just about to start his sixth performance when the train began to pull into the station.

'I wish you'd had a chance to question him,' Sheba said. 'We could have uncovered a clue as to who this Spider is, and where we could find them. Even why they want Mama Rat's map so badly.'

'You can walk back down the track and find him, if you like,' said Inji. 'Although you might need to sew him back together first.'

Sheba grimaced. 'I wasn't criticising you, Inji,' she said. 'Thank goodness you decided to follow after Remy. I had no idea that fellow was on our tail. I didn't pick up a scent, or anything.'

Remy wondered what she meant by 'scent'. It was the sound of the ticking that he had noticed. As far as he could tell, Thom hadn't smelt of anything, except perhaps engine oil.

His questions had to wait, though, as they began to climb down from the train, hauling all their luggage after them. He quickly pulled on his mask and gloves, then hopped out himself.

Dover station was right next to the sea, built out into the water. There was an arched roof over the train platform, and lots of official-looking buildings, bustling with people. But, beyond that, Remy spotted the sea. Stone breakwaters stretched out from the platform to create a manmade harbour, with piers jutting out even further among the waves. There were several tall-masted ships moored around the harbour walls, and a large packet steamer near to the platform. Streams of people were walking up ramps to board it, and pallets of goods were being loaded by crane. It looked smaller than the one Remy had stowed away on, but didn't have the same coating of rust and grime. The paintwork gleamed in the sunshine; white, red and shining gold.

'That's our boat,' said Sheba, pointing with her parasol. 'Why don't you all go and find our cabins. I just want to check the telegram office. Glyph said he might send us word if he uncovered anything.'

She walked off towards a squat brick building at the platform end, leaving the others to join the boarding queue with their luggage.

'Shouldn't someone go with her?' Remy suggested. He cast nervous glances at the crowds of passengers, all the while straining his ears for the tell-tale ticking of his enemies.

Pyewacket laughed. 'She doesn't need looking after. In fact, I almost feel sorry for anyone who tries messing with Sheba.'

'That's right,' said Inji. 'She makes me look like a pussycat.'

'You look like one of those, anyway,' said Pyewacket, before he could stop himself, and earned a slap on his bruised head. Remy watched the slight figure of Sheba walk across the platform, her wide skirts billowing behind her, and wondered what on earth made her so dangerous. Besides her gleaming amber eyes, she didn't even look Gifted, like the rest of them. If he hadn't seen that picture of her as a girl, covered with fur, he might have thought she was completely normal.

*

Once on board, they found their cabins. Two tiny rooms with double bunks in each. There was a porthole window, a small wardrobe to stow their clothes and not much else.

'We've got bigger cupboards than this in our kitchen,' Pyewacket complained, as he and Remy inspected their quarters.

'Stop moaning,' said Inji, her voice coming through the thin wooden wall. 'It's only for a few hours. We sail after supper and we'll be in Calais by dawn.'

Sheba found them, just as Remy was clambering up to the top bunk. She had a slip of paper in her hand: a telegram from London.

'It appears Glyph might have discovered who our metal-faced friend was,' she said, peering into the room. 'A man named George Thomas had a particularly nasty factory accident. Half of his face was destroyed, but he somehow survived. He was a bit of a medical curiosity for a while, and then turned to crime. He was arrested for burglary five years ago, but escaped. The Home Office believes he fled to France.'

'Sounds like our man,' said Pyewacket, kicking off his shoes and lying back on his bed. 'But at least he's out of action now.'

'That's true,' said Sheba. 'But there are four more henchmen out there, and they might have something in common with him. I've asked Glyph to look out for any other accident victims who have vanished recently.'

'Some of them spoke French,' Remy pointed out. 'They won't be in the British records, will they?'

'Possibly not,' said Sheba. 'But it's worth a try. Now I suggest we all have something to eat and then try and get some sleep. We're booked on the first train to Paris tomorrow morning.'

*

Sleep, as it turned out, was not to be had at all.

Pyewacket began to snore as soon as he curled in his blanket, but Remy lay on his bunk, his mind spinning with everything that had happened to him in such a short space of time.

Whenever he closed his eyes, he saw the mechanical face of Thom – or George Thomas, as he might once have been known – scowling at him, eyes filled with murderous fury. What could make a person so angry? What had Remy and his mother ever done to deserve such hate?

'I don't understand it, Pamplemousse,' he said to his china doll's head. 'Why can't people just be kind to each other?'

The doll, as usual, had no answer. Just a wobble of his last remaining eyeball.

Remy was still running through the attack, over

and over, when he felt the steamer cast off and begin to power itself through the water. The paddle smacked against the waves with a steady rhythm, and soon they were out on the open sea. Which was when the boat began to rock quite violently.

Perhaps his first crossing had been smooth because the goods ship was much bigger, or perhaps the waves had been calmer then. Either way, the rest of the voyage was nothing like his time in the merchant ship's hold. He spent endless hours being hurled from one side of his bunk to the other, crashing up against the cabin wall and then rolling to the edge and clinging on for dear life to stop himself tumbling down to the floor.

Through it all, the rumbling snore of Pyewacket echoed. Somehow, he managed to sleep like a baby. A very large, hairy baby in a thrashing, swinging crib.

When the ship finally pulled into the shelter of Calais harbour, Remy felt as though he had been churned by the craft's great steam wheel: smashed into froth like the wake of water that ran behind it. He staggered out of the cabin to find Inji and Sheba had slept just as badly. They both had dark rings beneath their eyes and were scowling like thunderstorms.

'Morning, all!' Pyewacket called from his bunk. 'What a delightful voyage that was! The best I've slept in ages. What's the matter with you lot? You look like somebody cancelled Christmas.'

'Do I have permission to knock him out again?' Inji muttered, under her breath.

'I'm seriously thinking about it myself,' Sheba replied.

*

The port at Calais was busier than Dover and Waterloo put together. Pyewacket paid a porter to take their luggage to the train station, and then they spent the rest of the morning getting their paperwork checked. Remy was surprised to notice that Sheba spoke very good French. He only had to help her with a couple of phrases.

When they were finally ready, they plunged into the bustle of people again, and made for the train.

One good thing about the press of travellers on all sides was that nobody had time to stare at them, or even notice they were different from the hundreds of other passengers. It did, however, make Remy very nervous. He strained his ears constantly, listening for any trace of clockwork noise. He imagined metal hooks and hands, snaking out from the crowd of bodies to grab him and pull him away. He pressed so close to Inji, he was practically hidden under her frock coat.

After much pushing and squeezing, they reached the train, checked their luggage was on board, and then clambered on themselves and began looking for an empty compartment in which they wouldn't be bothered. But, unlike last time, they found almost all the seats were taken. As they made their way along the crowded aisles, they got lots of strange looks.

Finally, tired of all the whispering and pointing, they had to settle for sharing a compartment with an elderly couple and a middle-aged businessman who constantly stared at them over the top of his newspaper, especially when Remy removed his mask. But the old lady was already asleep, and her husband had the thickest pair of spectacles Remy had ever seen. His eyesight must have been so bad, he probably thought they were just an everyday family from England, coming over for a spot of sightseeing.

He even began a conversation with Sheba, as the train eventually pulled out of the station. And continued chattering as they rolled and clacked through the French countryside.

Remy was sitting on the opposite seat, sandwiched in between Pyewacket and Inji. He soon felt a nudge in his ribs.

'What's the old guy saying to Sheba?' Pyewacket whispered, far too loudly.

'He's talking about why the train is so busy,' Remy replied. 'Apparently this is the last one to Paris for a while.'

'The last train? Why's that?' said Inji. She had been watching the old man with curious cat-eyes the whole time.

'Because of the war,' Remy translated. 'Louis Napoleon has surrendered and been captured by the Prussians. France is now a Republic again, and a man called Trochu is the president. But the war is still going on. The Prussian army is marching towards Paris. They think they will try and surround it until France admits defeat.'

'A siege?' said Pyewacket. 'Like they used to do to castles?'

Remy nodded.

'I don't understand,' said Inji. 'If they know Paris is going to be attacked, why are so many people heading *into* the city?'

'Well, this gentleman is going to stay with his daughter,' Remy explained. 'But he says many people think the siege will be exciting. They think the problems with the war were all because of Louis Napoleon being a bit of an idiot, and that now they have a new Republic, there's no way the Prussians can beat them.'

'They've done a pretty good job so far,' said Pyewacket. The businessman next to him huffed and rustled his newspaper, as if he had been offended.

'He says there are five hundred thousand soldiers of the National Guard inside Paris,' said Remy. 'And there are forts all around with many, many cannons. He says there is no way the Prussians can beat France. She has the most powerful army in Europe.'

'And what do you think?' Inji asked him. 'You used to live there. Can it be conquered?'

Remy shrugged. 'I don't imagine so,' he said. 'It's

a huge city. As big as London, at least, but much stronger. It has proper walls all around and a ring of forts outside that. It would take an enormous army to capture it.'

'Well, let's hope we're in and out before it comes to that,' said Pyewacket.

Remy agreed. And the thought that he might be with his mother again very soon, free and safe, filled him with a warm, peaceful feeling.

Squashed up between his two new friends, gently rocking as the train moved, his tired eyes couldn't stay open any longer. *I'm nearly there, Mother*, he managed to think, before he fell fast asleep.

CHAPTER NINE

In which Paris prepares for war.

Remy was woken by someone gently shaking his arm. He looked up through gritty eyes to see Inji bending over him.

'We're here,' she said. 'The "Guard ooh Norde", or whatever you call it.'

'Gare du Nord,' Remy mumbled, as he slipped his mask back on. From outside the train, he could hear the whoosh of steam and the roar of many voices, all shouting and talking at once.

'Well, whatever it is, the place has gone crazy. Look.'

Inji pointed out of the window, and Remy stood up to see. Sheba and Pyewacket were already on the platform, clinging tightly to their pile of luggage. All around them swept a sea of bodies. A chaos of people from every walk of Parisian life: shopkeepers, beggars, dandies, scholars, actors, dancers, waitresses, schoolchildren, grandparents, bakers and butchers. Each of them seemed to be going in their own direction, all pushing, shoving and milling around in a great whirlpool of noise and confusion.

'What's going on?' Remy said. He wondered if he might actually still be asleep, and all this was some kind of bad dream.

'It looks like half the city is trying to leave, and twice as many new folk are trying to get in,' said Inji. 'We're going to have to fight our way through. Hold tight to me, and don't let go!'

She lifted him down from the train and, taking a deep breath, they plunged into the throng, clinging tight to their luggage as they went.

Remy pushed Pamplemousse deep into his pocket and used both hands to cling on to Inji. She was squeezing him tight as well. He was sure he could feel the prickle of claws through her leather gloves.

The four of them, trunks and all, were swept up

and spun down the wide platform under its towering roof of glass and girders, towards the doors at the end. The guards and conductors had given up on checking tickets. They just stood back and let the wave of bodies pour out on to the streets, crashing up against others who were pushing in.

Remy and the others found themselves forced backwards – towards the train platforms rather than away – more than once but, finally, they broke out into daylight and on to a wide, open area outside.

There were still throngs of people everywhere, but most of them appeared to be in military uniform. Unlike the red-coated British soldiers Remy had glimpsed on the streets of London, these were all wearing navy blue, with crimson sashes around their waists. They wore matching crimson neckerchiefs and blue caps with stubby little peaks. All of them carried rifles with barrels almost as tall as them, and they stood in groups everywhere; smoking, drinking and laughing.

'These must be the National Guard that man was talking about,' said Sheba. 'There are hundreds of thousands of them in the city.'

Remy was about to ask where they were all

staying when he noticed rows of tents set up in the road. More soldiers were lounging around outside of them, looking as though they were on holiday rather than fighting in a war.

'Shouldn't they be off making barricades or something?' Pyewacket said. 'Don't they know the Prussians are coming?'

'Maybe they're just resting before the action starts,' said Sheba, not sounding very convinced. 'Come on, let's find ourselves somewhere to stay for the night.'

They began to make their way down the street, edging past camping soldiers and wagons stacked with supplies that were trundling slowly through the crowds. All the while, Remy scanned every face he passed, looking closely at their limbs for signs of machinery, listening out for the ticking of sinister clockwork. He knew the four remaining kidnappers were in this city somewhere, maybe the Spider as well. And it would be an impossible task to spot them among all these strangers. But at least, he supposed, the chaos would make it harder for them to be spotted as well.

The road soon opened out into an even wider

boulevard, but they were surprised to find it packed with sheep. The sound of bleating was deafening, and it stank like several hundred farmyards rolled into one.

'What's with all the mutton?' Pyewacket shouted, over the noise. 'Is this what it's usually like here?'

'No!' Remy shouted back. 'The sheep weren't here when I left! They must have brought them in for the siege!'

Fighting their way between makeshift pens and several flocks of escaped lambs, they managed to find a hotel on the Boulevard Rochechouart. It was a tall, three-storey building with ornate stonework that had seen better days. The paint was chipping from the shutters, and the windows needed a good clean. Still, it was somewhere that might have rooms, and a chance to escape the mayhem of the streets.

As they heaved their luggage through the doors, into the lobby, Remy noticed there were mounds of mattresses and blankets piled up at the foot of the staircase. Another group of those navy-clad soldiers were stacking some crates, the clinking of bottles coming from inside.

Something odd is happening here as well, Remy

thought. In the short time he had been away, the whole of Paris seemed to have transformed.

'Excuse me,' Sheba spoke in French to a lady behind the hotel desk. 'Do you have any rooms available?'

'Does it look like I do?' The lady gestured at the piles of crates and bedding all around her lobby, and the soldiers unpacking rolls of bandages. 'My business is now a hospital, apparently. By order of the new Republic! And all I get is a handful of francs for my trouble!'

She began to go red in the face, and looked as though she might burst into tears, so the Carnival quickly picked up their trunks and shuffled back on to the street.

The same thing happened in the next hotel they found. And the next. It seemed every building in sight was taken up somehow in the business of war.

'This is great,' said Pyewacket. 'Where are we supposed to sleep? In the gutter?'

Remy watched as a crew of soldiers cut down one of the beautiful trees on the side of the boulevard. It crashed to the ground in a shower of leaves, then they began to hack off the branches and drag it away. Behind it stretched a row of bare stumps. They seemed to be chopping down every tree in Paris; to help build barricades around the city, he supposed. 'I wish I'd been able to come down here before,' he said, thinking of his lonely life, stuck in his apartment. 'It must all have been beautiful.'

'What did you say, Remy?' Sheba had been watching the tree-felling as well. When she turned to him, her eyes were full of sadness, like his must be.

'Nothing,' he said. And then had an idea. 'We could go and stay in our old apartment. It's not far – we're right by Montmartre now.'

'That might not be safe,' said Inji. 'Those mechanical people know you used to live there. They could come back at any time.'

'What about the theatre Mama Rat was on about?' Pyewacket suggested. 'I bet they would put us up.'

'That's actually not a bad idea, for once,' said Inji. Pyewacket performed an extravagant bow.

'Do you know where it is, Remy?' Sheba asked.

Remy grimaced. He wasn't sure his mother would like him going there. But then again, where else could they turn? If only he knew his own city better ... he was as much a stranger here as these

Londoners. 'I think it's in Montmartre,' he said. 'But I'm not sure . . .'

Sheba put her hand on his shoulder. 'It will be fine, Remy. I promise. I know Sister Moon has bad memories of the place, but they will look after us. Our kind always stick together. We have to, so much of the time.'

'And we won't have to go far to find it,' said Inji. 'Look.'

She was pointing at the side of a nearby building, which had been covered in layer upon layer of posters and playbills. Most of them were washed blank by rain and bleached by the sun, but among the freshest layer was a print of a gnarled old man, a woman with two heads and what seemed to be a child with lobster claws. *Théâtre de Rêves*, it read. *20, Rue de Trois Frères, Montmartre.*

*

The road was a narrow, cobbled street with terraces of tall houses on either side, not unlike the one Remy and his mother had lived on. There were one or two cafés, a few shops and, of course, the theatre.

The building itself looked much the same as the others around it, but the window shutters had been painted with macabre and ghostly figures. Sinister beasts with horns and fangs, with wide green eyes and lolling tongues. The paint was faded and flaking, showing the grain of the warped wood underneath, an effect that somehow made the monsters look even more haunting and mysterious.

The theatre's name was painted on a hanging board above the front door that squeaked as it swung slowly in the autumn breeze. That was when Remy noticed this road, unlike the streets they had just passed through, was completely empty. The windows all around were blank, the shutters closed. A chill seemed to hang over the place, or was it just his imagination?

'Well, this place gives me the creeps,' said Pyewacket, clearly feeling the same.

'What does it mean?' Inji asked, pointing at the sign.

'Théâtre de Rêves,' said Remy. 'The Theatre of Dreams.'

'Nightmares, more like,' said Pyewacket. He shivered as Sheba walked up and knocked on the door.

There was silence for a long while. Long enough for Sheba to raise her knuckles to knock again – but then the sound of muffled footsteps came from somewhere within.

A few moments later, the door creaked open, revealing the hunched shape of the oldest man Remy had ever seen.

Bent over almost double, he had a bald head to which a few strands of white hair clung, like straggly trees on a mountainside.

His face was a mass of wrinkles upon wrinkles upon wrinkles; they criss-crossed over each other, the skin as thin as tissue paper. Tufty white eyebrows sprang out above a pair of watery-blue eyes and a long, hooked nose. His mouth was lost in a beard that hung down so far, it dragged along the floor.

'*Oui?*' he said, his voice faint and wheezy.

'Excuse us,' said Sheba, in her best French. 'We were told by our friend Marie, that . . .'

The old man held up a knobbly hand, cutting her off. He was staring at Remy as if he had seen a ghost. Remy blinked back, peering through the smoked lenses of his mask. Did this man recognise him? Without even seeing his face?

'Why does that one wear a hood?' the old man asked, speaking in English.

'He's allergic to the sun,' replied Sheba. 'And how did you know I was English?'

'Your French is terrible,' said the man.

'Oh yes?' Pyewacket bristled, defensive. 'And who taught you English? William Shakespeare?'

'Actually, I taught *him*.' The old man winked. 'Couldn't string a sentence together when I first met him.' He turned his attention back to Remy. 'Tell me, child. Do you have scarlet eyes? And two sharp teeth?'

Remy swallowed hard, and then nodded.

'Remiel!' The old man clasped his hands together. 'We have been expecting your return! Lisette saw it in her cards. But where is Zara? Your mother?'

Remy opened his mouth to say something, but all that came out was a strangled sob. It was all too much: Paris turned into a war zone, the hordes of people and now this mysterious old man, talking to him as though he was a long-lost grandfather . . .

Inji put a protective arm around his shoulders and glared at the old man, daring him to upset Remy further. 'She's in trouble. We've come to help her,' she said, her voice low and dangerous.

'It's very upsetting for Remy,' Sheba explained.

'Of course, of course.' The old man nodded his head. His neck was so wizened and scrawny, it looked like it might snap from the sudden movement. 'Come in, please. Any help we can give Zara will be freely given. And Remiel – this place is as good as your home. You were born within its very walls, you know.'

He stepped back and beckoned them inside. With more than a little relief at finding a safe haven, the Carnival picked up their trunks and walked into the musty darkness of the theatre.

CHAPTER TEN

*In which Remy hears the
truth about his father.*

They stepped into a foyer not unlike that of
the hotels they had just visited. Except this
one had the shutters firmly closed, making the light
dim and murky. The deep shadows instantly soothed
Remy. He pulled off the stifling mask and wiped the
tears from his eyes. Inji reached down to brush his
long hair back over his ears as he looked at his new
surroundings.

They stood in a carpeted area, with a ticket desk
at one end. Posters of various acts hung here and
there. One looked like the old man who had let
them in, another was the two-headed woman they

had seen on the playbill. The walls were covered in flocked paper: midnight blue with circles and swirls of gold. It may have looked impressive once, but the effect was ruined by bubbles of damp and creeping blotches of mould. There was a thick smell of dust and mildew that stuck in Remy's throat. And underneath it, the unmistakable scent of mouse droppings. This theatre had clearly seen much better days.

'Welcome,' said the old man. 'My name is Methuselah, the oldest human being in the world – at least as far as my act is concerned. I already know Remiel, but I am afraid the rest of you have me at a disadvantage.'

Sheba politely introduced herself and the others, then gave a brief explanation of how they came to be there. 'We were wondering,' she added, 'if we might stay here for a few nights, while we try to locate Sister Moon. We shall pay you for the inconvenience, of course.'

'I shall not take a penny!' Methuselah looked offended. 'I remember Marie, her rats and her strong companion well. Any friends of theirs are friends of ours too. And we will do everything in our power to help rescue poor Zara. You may stay as long as you like – the city is a peculiar place for visitors at the moment; times of war are always so bothersome, and they seem to happen every five minutes in this country. Come, I will take you through to the living quarters. There are only a few of us who have decided to stay and brave the oncoming attack, I'm afraid.'

After pausing to smile at Remy's unmasked face, he led them behind the ticket desk and through a door into the theatre's backstage area. They emerged in a small room with bare walls of cracked plaster. Dressing tables with large mirrors were pushed up against the sides, their surfaces covered with pots of make-up and glass jars stuffed full of brushes. A flickering gaslight on the wall gave the place a dim glow. Through the open door opposite, Remy could see the curtains of the stage itself. They were pulled shut, and the space in between was packed with rolls of canvas and pieces of wooden scenery. Ropes hung down from the darkness above like vines in the jungle. On the other side, he knew, there would be rows and rows of seats for the audience.

'This is where the magic is prepared,' said Methuselah, gesturing at the tables and a large wardrobe in the corner, which Remy guessed must be full of costumes. 'Can you feel it in your blood, Remiel? Your parents were born performers. They lived for the cheers of the crowd, the gasps of astonishment . . .'

'That's not how *I* remember being put on show,' said Inji, her lip curled. 'I had to stand and be gawked at by a bunch of drunken yobs every night, just because I looked different. Remy's lucky he hasn't had to go through all that.'

'Yes,' said Pyewacket. 'We all had a hard time of it, Sister Moon included. I don't blame her for keeping Remy away.'

Methuselah shook his head sadly. 'Ah, my brothers and sisters,' he said. 'I understand your dislike of the stage. This place was a similar affair – a sideshow, I believe you call it – before we took it over for ourselves. Since then, we have made it our own. We perform works of art, and our audience appreciates them for their beauty and mystery. There is no drunken "gawking" here.'

Remy looked around at the dressing tables, the

lights, the curtains. His father would have sat at one of those chairs, looked at himself in one of the mirrors. Perhaps some of those brushes had actually touched his face. He would have walked out on those very floorboards every night, waiting for the show to begin. Until ... the accident. Whatever it had been – his mother had never really talked about it. But *here* was someone who knew. Who had been there at the time. The thought filled him with a sudden desire, as bright and hot as a burning sun.

'Mister Methuselah,' he said. 'My father ... what happened to him? Why did my mother leave your theatre and never come back?'

'Ah.' Methuselah fidgeted with his long beard. 'That is a long and sad story. And one your mother obviously didn't think you were ready for. I'm not sure it is my place to tell it.'

'Please.' Remy reached out to grasp one of the old man's gnarled hands. It was like holding a twisted tree branch, wrapped around in ancient leather. 'I've asked her and asked her, but she won't ... she *can't* tell. But he was my father. I *have* to know. I have a right to, don't I?'

Methuselah looked long and hard at Remy, as if reading the inside of his mind. Finally, he nodded.

'I suppose you do, young man. Although I regret being the one to tell you. Perhaps we should head upstairs to the kitchen. We shall sit around the table, break bread together and I will spin the tale.'

*

The kitchen was at the very top of the building, up a narrow servants' staircase that zigged and zagged and nearly gave Pyewacket a heart attack as he heaved up the largest of the trunks.

When they had stacked their luggage in the corridor, Methuselah led them into a small room with a single grubby window. They all sat around a dining table on rickety chairs as the old man laid out some crusty bread, a slab of butter and some chipped wine glasses. He pulled a dusty bottle of red wine from a cabinet and uncorked it, pouring them all a glassful.

'I suppose,' he said, taking a seat, 'I should start when your mother arrived, Remiel. In those days, the theatre was owned by a showman. An unpleasant bully, as most showmen tend to be, who treated all his acts little better than animals.

'I believe he knew this Plumpscuttle fellow, who ran a similar show in London. Carnival of something or other . . .'

'Carnival of the Lost,' said Pyewacket, puffing out his chest.

'That's the badger,' said Methuselah. 'Well, Zara – Sister Moon – was shipped across from that establishment, and soon became the star act here. She would stand on stage, the theatre lights would go out, then flicker on again, and she would be in the back row of the audience. Travelling the span of the room in the blink of an eye. In the speed of a wink. The crowd loved her.

'For many years, she missed her home and friends terribly. But then a young man was brought here from India. *Le Serpent*, they called him, but his real name was Azad.

'He had a skin affliction, you see. Dry and leathery, overlapping in patches. It made it look as though he had scales. And there were his teeth too, of course. He had fangs – like yours, Remiel, but much bigger – and they carried poison.

'The showman spun the usual rubbish about him: his mother had been bitten by a cobra when she was expecting. His father was strangled by a boa constrictor ... the story changed every time. Azad hated it all terribly, and was very homesick. Until he met Zara, that is. The two of them were a great comfort to each other, and they soon became married. Not long after that, young Remiel was born.

'We were all so happy for them – the other acts, at least. Our owner had different ideas. He saw the whole thing as a way to earn money. He was constantly trying to make them bring the baby out on stage for the crowd to see.

'There was a lot of interest, you understand, from newspapers and the like. Word had got out about Remiel's crimson eyes and his teeth. About his allergy to the sun. You can imagine what nonsense was published about him. And some most unpleasant people heard about it, of course. I'm sure you've all come across them: nasty folk who don't like our kind because we look different. And these ones believed there was a vampire in Paris. They actually thought a tiny, harmless baby was going to drain them all of blood in their sleep.

'We had several stones thrown through our windows. Rude words painted on the door, things like that. But one night, a large group of them came into the theatre. They sat in the audience – our owner was too cowardly to turn them away – and shouted horrible things about Azad, Zara and Remiel all through the show.

'Finally, they demanded to see the baby. They even threatened to burn the theatre down if he wasn't brought out. Zara refused, of course, but our owner threatened to turn her and Azad out on to the streets if she didn't do what they wanted and, knowing how difficult it would be to become homeless with a small child, she reluctantly agreed. I think, perhaps, she also hoped they might see how tiny and innocent the babe was and stop all their nonsense.

'But it was not to be. No sooner had the crib appeared, than the hateful louts stormed on to the stage, yelling things about holy water and crosses and curses. One of them managed to grab Zara's hair and throw her to the floor. She cried out, frightened they might harm the baby. At this point Azad became so terrified, he tried to defend his wife. Before he could control himself, he bit the brute who had manhandled her. Poisoned him with his venom.

'Although brave, it was the worst possible thing he could have done. The police were called and, even though the man survived, Azad was arrested and tried for attempted murder.

'You can imagine how little sympathy he got. A person who looked so different, from another country as well ... He was found guilty and sentenced to death.'

Remy's jaw hung open. He dimly realised he was shaking his head as he heard all this. He'd always thought there had been a terrible accident: a fall, a fire, something like that. But his father had died because he was protecting *him*. Which meant, in a way, that it was *his* fault ...

'I know what you're thinking, Remiel.' Methuselah was peering at him again, looking into his very soul. 'But it was absolutely *not* your fault. Blame the law, blame the spiteful idiots for hating anyone who doesn't look like them ... blame everyone in the theatre if you like, for not doing more to stop it ... but you must not blame yourself.'

Sheba took one of his hands and Inji the other.

They held tight while tears began to spill down his cheeks.

'What happened to the showman?' Pyewacket asked, after the silence had stretched on long enough. 'He doesn't seem to be here now. How did you get rid of him?'

Methuselah sighed. 'After the attack, there was a scandal. Our doors had to close, and the debts quickly piled up. Over my many, many years, I had managed to gather quite an amount of gold, so I offered to buy the place. On the condition that the showman left France and never returned. To my great sorrow, Zara did not want to be a part of it. There were too many painful memories for her here. She left to hide herself and you, Remiel, from the cruel world.'

'So you've been running the theatre ever since?' Sheba asked.

'I have.' Methuselah smiled. 'And we have turned it into something other than a cheap sideshow. Or we had, before this pesky war came along. But wars end, eventually. We will be up and running again as soon as it is over.'

Remy took a deep, shuddering breath. Now he

knew the truth, he realised he wanted his mother back more than ever. He was all she had in the world. All those years, tucked away in that apartment, not allowing him any freedom, any friends. It suddenly made sense.

'We need to find her,' he whispered. 'We need to rescue her.'

Sheba put her arm around him. 'Soon,' she said. 'First we must find the map.'

'Have you tried alerting the authorities?' Methuselah asked. 'I know the city is in chaos at the moment, but they might still want to catch a gang of kidnappers.'

Inji snorted. 'Do you really think they would listen to Remy? Or any of us? They'd take one look at us and laugh their socks off. Besides, if this Spider is as clever as we think, they will have moved Sister Moon somewhere else as soon as they found out Remy had escaped.'

Methuselah nodded. 'Perhaps you're right. Although it wouldn't hurt to check. There may even be a clue as to where they have gone. Can you remember where it was you were held captive, Remiel?'

Remy thought back to that night. To climbing out of the cellar window and running down the street with Pamplemousse clutched tightly in both hands. There had been a street sign, hadn't there? He closed his eyes to remember better.

'Rue Chapon,' he said, seeing it loom in his memory. 'The house with a grille in the ground in front of it, above the cellar windows.'

'Very good,' said Methuselah. 'The young cat-lady may be right, but it wouldn't hurt to check. I have just the fellow for the job, as well.'

As they watched, Methuselah walked to the kitchen door and called out. A few moments later footsteps could be heard, and two figures walked in to join them.

The first was an old lady, draped in a hooded purple cloak. A thatch of coarse grey hair hung down past her shoulders and wide but kind brown eyes stared out from a wrinkled face. There was a large bulge on the right side of the cloak, as if she was carrying something hidden in her arms. It twitched and moved – a child, maybe? Or a pet?

The second person was a young boy. Young, but incredibly tall. He towered over everyone in the room, his head almost brushing the ceiling. When Remy looked closer, he could see that the boy's limbs were much longer than they should be. Thin as sticks, it looked as though he had been stretched out like a lump of toffee. His hands were like flapping pink spiders, and each digit had a silver ring on the end. As he moved his fingers, Remy noticed that the rings had hooks attached, for some reason. *Does he use them to catch fish?* Remy wondered. *They do look a bit like wiggling earthworms.*

'May I introduce Lisette and Verlaine,' said Methuselah. 'The last remaining members of our troupe.'

The two gave nervous bows, their eyes flicking over the Carnival and seeming to linger on Remy more than the others. He wondered if they had known his father too. Whether they had any stories about him.

'Verlaine, I have a job for you,' said Methuselah. 'Go to the Rue Chapon and look into any cellar windows you find. There's a chance a young woman might be held captive there. She has long black hair, and eyes to match. Make sure you aren't seen.'

The tall youth nodded and left the room. As he

walked, Remy noticed he had hooked rings on the toes of his bare feet as well. They made tiny tapping sounds as they clicked against the floorboards.

'That boy is an astonishing climber,' Methuselah explained. 'He can reach anywhere in Paris without ever touching the ground. It's like watching an insect walk up a pane of glass. Amazing. He'll be back shortly, and we'll know if Zara is still trapped there.'

'I don't hold out much hope,' said Sheba. 'But thank you, anyway. And tomorrow we need to enter the catacombs. There's an item hidden there that we hope to trade for Sister Moon. Are they still a tourist attraction?'

'Ah.' Methuselah tugged at his beard. 'I'm afraid the catacombs have been sealed off as part of the preparations for the siege. I read about it in the news, just this morning. You shall have to engage in a spot of breaking and entering.'

'That's one of our specialities,' Pyewacket said, grinning.

'I'm sure it is,' said Methuselah, raising an eyebrow. 'Perhaps, then, you should have an early night. Rest yourselves for your adventure on the morrow.'

'That's the best idea I've heard all day.' Pyewacket drained the rest of his wine and stifled a burp. The others began to rise from the table too. Remy was about to disagree and suggest heading straight to the catacombs. He didn't want to waste a second sleeping. But then he noticed the sky through the kitchen window. It had already started to dim to a bruise-purple. As much as he belonged to the night, even he didn't fancy walking through an underground, skull-filled labyrinth at the very time ghosts, ghouls and phantoms were about.

'This way,' said Lisette, the old woman, speaking for the first time. Her voice was high and reedy, but soft. For some reason, Remy could imagine it singing lullabies. He followed as she led them out of the kitchen and along the corridor.

They passed a series of rooms, the open doors revealing unused beds; bare mattresses with sagging springs and sad, stained pillows. It looked as though, at one time, many people might have called the Théâtre de Rêves home. *Which room had been his parents'*, he wondered? *The very place he was born.*

Lisette stopped them halfway along the corridor. She gestured to the doors on either side. 'You can take these rooms,' she said. 'Mine and Verlaine's are the next ones down, if you need anything in the night.'

'Thank you,' said Sheba, helping Inji to fetch their trunk and take it through to one of the bedrooms. Remy was about to walk into the opposite one, when Lisette stopped him with a hand on his shoulder.

'I'm glad you came back,' she said, smiling at him. 'I don't suppose you remember Noisette and I.' She gently lifted a corner of her cloak to reveal a small creature, the size of a toddler but with a face as wrinkled as Lisette's. Its arms were wrapped around the old woman's neck and it opened one sleepy eye to stare at Remy. He was about to ask why she was carrying it like a baby when he noticed that its chest was joined to Lisette's. The pair were fused together: twins who had been born sharing one body.

'I ... uh ...' He didn't know what to say. There *was* something familiar about them, but he couldn't put his finger on it. 'Did I know you when I was a baby?'

'You did!' Lisette beamed, and even the sleepy Noisette managed a smile. 'We were the ones who delivered you. We used to help look after you. Sing you to sleep and feed you your bottles.'

'Thank you,' Remy smiled back at them. 'That was very kind.'

'It was our pleasure.' Lisette held the door open for him. 'We loved your mother and father very much. We hope you find her again.'

'So do I,' whispered Remy. Feeling squashed full of old memories and new discoveries, he trudged into his room.

*

Sheba found him at the window, clutching Pamplemousse, looking down at the empty street below; just as he had sat, night after night, in the tiny apartment he shared with his mother. Except now everything was different. The sounds, the smells . . . there was a constant babble of noise coming from the city: animals bleating, singing, chanting – it seemed Paris couldn't make up its mind whether it was partying or panicking.

'Are you all right, Remy?' He heard Sheba's voice behind him, but didn't look round. He didn't want her to see he had been crying. Again.

'Yes,' he lied. 'Just, you know . . . thinking . . .'

Sheba came and sat next to him on the windowsill. The glow of the gas lamp on the wall caught her eyes, making them gleam orange, like flaming embers were trapped inside.

'It must have been hard,' she said. 'Hearing that about your father.'

Remy gave a little shrug. 'I knew there had been an accident,' he said. 'But not ...' He found he couldn't speak the words. As if saying them would make it real, somehow.

'I heard the truth about my parents when I was about your age,' Sheba said. 'It was a great shock to me as well. Everything I had thought or guessed about them, shattered in an instant.'

'Did they die too?' Remy asked.

Sheba nodded. 'My father died alone, of an illness. My mother passed away in the workhouse, leaving me to be taken in by a horrid sideshow owner. Neither of them ever really knew me. Perhaps they loved me, in the short time we had. I like to think so.'

'Oh, Sheba.' Remy reached out to take her hand. 'I'm so sorry.'

'It's all right,' she replied. 'I have my friends around me. They are all the family I ever need. I count myself very lucky. And you are too. Your mother must love you very much. And your father . . . that was a very brave thing he did.'

'I just don't understand. Why do people hate us so much? Can it really be just because we look different?'

Sheba sighed. 'I've spent many hours wondering about that myself. And I never get close to an answer. I think it's because they have spent so much time and effort building a society where they can be safe, where they can have all their little luxuries . . . but to be a part of it you have to play by the rules. Dress a certain way, talk a certain way, think a certain way. And anybody who doesn't fit in threatens all that. They're terrified of anything different, because it might mess up their perfect little world.'

'It's so unfair.' Remy looked across the street, where a lone black cat was padding across a rooftop. 'It means people who look like us can never be welcome. And it's not *our* fault. We can't change how we look.'

'It isn't fair at all,' Sheba agreed. 'Perhaps one day the world will learn to judge people by how kind they are, not how pretty.'

Remy laughed. 'I don't think that will ever happen.' They sat and watched the cat slink between the chimneys until it disappeared into the darkness.

CHAPTER ELEVEN

*In which the Carnival
enter the catacombs.*

After another night of listening to Pyewacket snoring, Remy was awoken by voices coming from along the corridor. He quickly dressed and skipped down to the kitchen, leaving his noisy roommate snorting and gurgling.

He found Methuselah at the table, pouring coffee for Sheba and Inji. Verlaine had returned and was telling them about what he had found.

'There were two houses on the Rue Chapon with cellar windows,' he said, in French. 'Both of them were empty. I even crept inside. Nobody was home.'

Remy's heart sank. Now his mother could be *anywhere* in the city. Even if they found the map, they would then face the impossible task of locating her. Unless, of course, the Spider and their crew found them first.

'Just as we thought,' said Sheba. 'But thank you for checking.'

'There is more news,' Verlaine said. 'The Prussians have arrived. They are setting up guns around the city. The siege has begun.'

'That's going to make things tricky,' said Inji, once Sheba had translated. 'How are we going to get back home again? We could be stuck here for months.'

'We'll cross that bridge when we come to it. We have a map and a friend to find first. Good morning, Remy.' Sheba had spotted him in the doorway and pulled him out a chair. Methuselah handed him a cup of steaming coffee and a plate of hot, buttered croissants.

'Are we going to the catacombs today?' he asked, biting into one of the flaky pastries.

'As soon as we are all up and ready,' said Sheba. Remy noticed she had changed into a practical-looking dress. It still had wide skirts and a bow of ribbon at the neck, but there were pockets sewn on to the chest and arms. A belt at her waist held various pouches, from one of which poked the wooden handle of her clockwork pistol.

'Somebody had better go and wake Pyewacket up, or we'll be waiting until midnight,' said Inji. Remy could see she was wearing the bulletproof waistcoat that Sheba had designed. A black canvas backpack sat on the table, full – he expected – of adventuring equipment.

Remy finished his breakfast as fast as he was able, hot coffee scalding his tongue. By the time the grumbling Pyewacket was forced out of bed, he was ready in his mask and gloves. 'Today is the day,' he whispered to Pamplemousse. 'We're going to save Mother!'

*

'Here we are,' said Sheba, as their carriage pulled up between two matching pavilions made of sandy-yellow stone. 'The Barrière d'Enfer. The Toll Gate of Hell.'

'We're going into hell?' Pyewacket's face went pale behind his whiskers.

'Not really.' Sheba gave a nervous laugh. 'At least I hope not. It's what they used to call these buildings when they were a gateway into the city.'[viii]

'Where are the catacombs?' Remy asked. He had been expecting a grand entrance to a hidden, bone-filled underworld. Some kind of flaming gate, perhaps, with skull-topped pillars. Instead, Sheba pointed to a humble little black-painted building, hardly bigger than a shed, tacked on to the side of the eastern pavilion.

'Is that it?' Pyewacket said, unimpressed. 'It should take us about five minutes to find this secret skull, then. Not a very good hiding place.'

'The catacombs are *underground*, stupid,' said Inji.

'Yes, they stretch for many miles underneath the city,' said Sheba. 'The part with the bones in is only a tiny section. We could be searching for a while.'

It was already nearly midday. They had left the theatre straight after breakfast, but it had taken them a long time to find a carriage that would drive them to the south of the city, and even longer for their ride to pick its way through the crowded streets. Then they had stopped at a telegraph office, to see if Glyph had sent any further word, only to discover that the lines had been cut by the Prussians. There was no way of communicating with anyone outside of Paris now.

The city's mood seemed to have changed since the day before. The crowds of National Guard and citizens they passed were more serious, more grim. Everybody seemed to be waiting for the sound of Prussian cannon fire to begin, for buildings around them to fly apart, or explosions to rip through the streets. Squads of troops were marching here and there, but without any real purpose. It was as if everyone thought they should be fighting, but nobody knew exactly who to attack or where they should be doing it.

'There are soldiers on the entrance,' Remy pointed out. Two guardsmen were leaning up against the building wall. One appeared to be sleeping, the other was picking stones from the sole of his boot with a knife.

'How are we going to deal with them?' Inji asked. 'Tranquilliser darts? Slip them some poison? Or just stroll up and knock them out with a bit of lead pipe?'

'Nothing so drastic,' Sheba said. 'I've been watching these guardsmen, and it appears most of them aren't really trained soldiers. And they seem very fond of their wine. Wait here a moment.'

Opening her parasol, she strolled over to them and began to talk to the one cleaning his shoe. After a few moments he began smiling and laughing. Remy strained his ears to hear what they were saying, but they were too far away. He saw Sheba shake hands with the guard, then he nudged his comrade awake and the pair walked off down the street. Sheba beckoned them all over.

'What did you say to them?' Remy asked, amazed.

'I expect she hypnotised them,' said Pyewacket.

'Of course not!' Sheba laughed. 'I simply pretended to be a British tourist, desperate to see the catacombs. They wouldn't let me in, but I offered them some money and told them that a wine seller down the street was selling cheap drinks to celebrate the siege beginning. Then they said I could have an hour to myself among the bones. They even gave me the key!'

She held up a heavy iron key, and then used it to unlock the thick oak doors. Pyewacket looked a little disappointed. 'That was easy,' he said. 'What are we going to tell them, though, when they've finished mafficking[ix] about and you come back up with all of us in tow?'

'We'll deal with that later,' said Sheba. She swung open the door to reveal a small room. A rack of unlit bullseye lanterns stood against the wall, underneath a large, printed map. In the centre, filling almost all the floor, was the top of a wide spiral staircase.

'Shall we descend?'

Remy followed the others inside. The door swung shut behind them, instantly cutting off the bright gleam of daylight, and plunging them all into darkness. He pulled off his mask and breathed deeply, feeling the cool pull of the shadows on his skin and, leaching out from the staircase, the quiet song of deep, ancient, lightless caverns.

'It's pitch-black in here!' Pyewacket moaned. 'Shall we grab one of those lanterns?'

'No need,' said Sheba. 'I have a much less noticeable one.' There was a flash of light as she struck a match, and then a dim red glow appeared. She held up a fist-sized lamp with panes of coloured glass. Her eyes reflected the gleam in twin points of orange. 'This should be enough for us to navigate by.'

'For you, Inji and Remy, maybe,' said Pyewacket. 'But *I* don't have freaky night-eyes, remember? How am I supposed to see where I'm going?'

'Put these on.' Inji had her backpack open. She handed Pyewacket the pair of steel-rimmed goggles with bulbous eyepieces. He slipped them over his head, making him look like some kind of giant fanged toad with oversized arms. 'I can see!' he shouted, his voice echoing all around them.

'Hush!' hissed Sheba. And then, 'Light-sensitive lenses. Don't say I never get you anything. Now, lead on, Inji.'

They began to head down the stone steps, curling deeper and deeper into the ground. The light from Sheba's lantern painted everything red, but to Remy's eyes it was as clear as daylight. He could see the joins of every brick, scrawls of names and dates on the wall, the worn edges of the steps where thousands of booted feet had rubbed them smooth over time.

Down they went, round and round, further and further, until the air became cold, damp and tinged with staleness. The smell of dead things: dust and bone and rot. They walked for so long, Remy began to think they might never stop. That they might end up coming out on the other side of the world.

'Last step,' whispered Inji. She took the lantern from Sheba and held it up to reveal a long tunnel, stretching off from the foot of the stairs, into the distance. The walls were rough-hewn blocks, the floor bare stone. An arched ceiling ran above, upon which somebody had painted a thick black line with the odd arrow, showing them which way to go. There were gaslight sconces – unlit – dotted here and there. It was just wide enough for them to walk along in single file.

'Where are the bones?' Remy spoke in a whisper too. Something about the darkness and the emptiness made it seem wrong to talk any louder.

'We have to walk a little way to find the ossuary,' Sheba explained. 'Methuselah told me how to reach the Samaritan's Fountain. It's a fair bit in.'

'How does he know where it is?' Remy asked. He couldn't imagine that frail old man managing those steps, let alone wandering around in the dark down here.

'He said he helped build it, three hundred odd years ago. When this place was a limestone quarry. He certainly seemed to know a lot about it.'

'Probably just read a guidebook,' said Pyewacket, with a sniff. 'I don't buy all this "oldest man in the world" nonsense. It's just a stupid story to make his act seem more interesting.'

'What, like pretending to be a witch's imp with magic powers?' Inji grinned in the dark. Remy could see points of light flickering on her sharp teeth.

'I was just a young, foolish lad back then,' said Pyewacket, with a pout. 'That leathery old trout should know better.'

Still bickering, they headed down the long tunnel.

*

As they went along the passage, Remy began to walk as close to Inji as he could, even though it meant brushing up against the crumbly stone. At one point he even slipped a hand into hers. Did she feel the walls beginning to close in, like he did? Was she afraid of the moment they would step out of the tunnel and finally see the skeletons? She gave his hand a little squeeze and looked down at him with a reassuring smile. She didn't seem scared at all.

The smell of old bone grew steadily stronger the further they went. Sheba pulled a handkerchief from her pocket and pressed it over her nose, as if she felt it more than anyone else.

'We're here,' she said, through the kerchief, as they stepped into an open chamber. Pillars, painted with striking black-and-white patterns, held up the stone roof and opposite them was a low doorway, decorated on either side with a white-on-black diamond. Words were carved on the lintel above it.

'*Arrête!*' read Inji. '*C'est ici L'Empire de la Mort.*'

'Halt,' translated Remy. 'This here is the Empire of Death.'

'I've been thinking,' said Pyewacket, his voice trembling just a little. 'We don't even need this map. Not really. I can track down these villains with my incredible sleuthing skills, then Inji can do her cat-thing and scratch them all into ribbons. Then we can rescue Moonie and be back in London Town before teatime. Easy as biscuits.'

Inji snorted. 'There's a ten-year-old here who's less frightened than you.'

Remy felt Pyewacket's goggled eyes turn to stare at him, and tried to look as brave as possible. The truth was, if it wasn't for the chance of saving his mother, you wouldn't find him down here for all the tea in China.

'Through we go, then,' said Sheba.

The adults had to duck their heads to pass through the doorway. Still clinging to Inji's hand, Remy followed, with Pyewacket bringing up the rear. They found themselves in a corridor with strange patterns on the walls. Rows and rows of small bumps and knobbles, with the occasional line of melon-sized domes. It was only after they had walked a few metres that Remy realised what he was actually seeing.

'Bones!' he squeaked.

'Napoleon's knickers!' he heard Pyewacket curse behind him.

The criss-crossing decoration was made by the ends of thigh bones, stacked on top of each other, from the floor to the ceiling. And the domes, of course, were skulls. They poked out, staring into the corridor with their gaping, empty eye sockets, the gaps in their jaws where their teeth had fallen out, the triangular holes that were once noses.

'How . . . how many?' Inji said. Even she sounded a little shaken.

'There's about six million bodies down here,' Sheba said, through her handkerchief. 'The contents of the city's cemeteries for several hundred years.'

His mother had described it to him, but it was nothing like what he had imagined. No wonder the ancient cemeteries had been bursting at the seams. So many people, so much death. He had always thought, staring down from his attic window, that Paris was a place teeming with life. And all the time, it had really been a city of the dead.

'Look.' Pyewacket was pointing at the wall. 'They've made a heart shape out of skulls! Was someone having a laugh?'

'I think it's quite powerful,' said Sheba. 'Every one of these skeletons was a person once. They all fell in love, in one way or another. Imagine the sheer amount of it that was felt and given, over time, by everyone in these catacombs.'

'I bet they never thought they'd end up as wallpaper for an underground dungeon, though,' said Inji. 'Which way is the fountain? I want to get out of here as soon as possible.'

Sheba pointed ahead. 'It's the first turning on the right,' she said. 'Methuselah said we can't miss it.'

'Let's hope not,' said Pyewacket. 'Imagine getting lost down here and starving to death.'

That's exactly what Remy was trying *not* to imagine. He clutched Pamplemousse in his pocket and followed the others down the passageway.

*

The bones carried on, lining both sides of the corridor, with no signs of ever stopping. Remy gazed at the endless rows of skulls as he passed, trying to imagine them as people. What kind of lives had they had? What jobs, what families, what adventures? Those hollow cradles once held thoughts and dreams and fears, just like *his* head did now. *I will be a skull too, one day*, he thought. *And then there will be no difference between me and everybody else.* How silly it seemed – down here where everyone who lived had been rendered the same – to treat people differently, just because of a thin layer of muscle and skin.

'This is it!' said Sheba, making everyone jump.

Remy had been staring at the bones so intently, he hadn't noticed they'd turned the corner. Now they were standing in a wide room, in the centre of which was a circular, stone pool. It had a wall around it, high at the back and descending in steps to ground level at the front. The inside was filled with icy-looking water. A lone goldfish, its scales and eyes turned blank white from living in the dark, swam in endless circles, softly popping bubbles escaping from its lips.

Poor thing, Remy thought. *Down here alone, in the dark, with only the dead for company.*

'Oh, look,' said Pyewacket, grinning. 'Someone left supper for Inji.'

Inji made a point of ignoring him. 'So, it could be in any one of these?' she said, looking around the room. There were three rows of skulls at different heights: top, middle and bottom. They circled the chamber completely, at least three hundred of them.

'It has this symbol on it,' said Remy. He took the piece of paper Mama Rat gave him and unfolded it for everyone to see.

'Well, I can't see *anything* written on *any* of these bone-boxes,' said Pyewacket.

'It could be quite small,' said Sheba. 'We're going to have to search. Remy, take the bottom ones, Pye: the middle. Inji and I will do the top. Spread out and get looking.'

As Pyewacket began to grumble, Remy crouched down and peered at the skulls on the bottom row. It felt rude, somehow, staring so closely at the insides of these long-dead Parisians' heads. He found himself murmuring 'sorry' as he carefully examined each one.

The search took many long, cold minutes, there in the underground fountain chamber. Everything was silent, except the occasional flip of the blind goldfish's tail and the scuff of boots on gravel as they inched their way around the room.

Remy was almost halfway along his row when he spotted it. The tiniest symbol painted in red ink just above the left eye of a yellowed skull.

'I think I've found it,' he whispered. He pulled the paper from his pocket again to double check. It was a definite match.

There was a scrabble of footsteps as everyone rushed over.

'Where's the map, then?' Pyewacket said. The

skull looked just the same as any other. Toothless, crumbling. Bone as yellow and brittle as old parchment.

'Look in the mouth,' suggested Inji.

'No, the eye,' said Sheba. 'Can you get your fingers inside, Remy? You have the smallest hands.'

Remy looked up at her in horror, but she was deadly serious. He swallowed hard, then reached his fingers into the empty socket.

Sorry, sorry, sorry, he repeated in his head. He couldn't help but imagine what had once sat where his fingertips were poking. A plump, juicy eyeball, rolling around. It would be looking up at him in fury.

'I can't feel anything,' he said, starting to draw his hand back.

'Try at the back of the socket,' Sheba suggested. 'There's a gap where the optic nerve joins the brain. It might be in there.'

'Really?' The thought of touching the actual skull made Remy's stomach turn. But if they didn't find the map . . .

This is for you, Mother, he thought, reaching deeper and brushing his fingers around until he felt it: the crinkly edge of a rolled-up piece of paper – just the end, poking out from a gap in the bone.

'Got it,' he said, through gritted teeth. He trapped the roll between his two fingers and began to slowly pull it out.

'Careful,' said Pyewacket. 'It's been in there for over twenty years. I expect it's pretty delicate.'

Bit by tiny bit, Remy eased the paper out until it popped free with a tiny crackling noise. A thin tube, no longer than his little finger. He held the roll up for them all to see. 'Shall I open it?'

'Of course!' Pyewacket was almost hopping up and down with excitement. 'Let's find out where the necklace is hidden, then we can swap the map for Moonie *and* run off to nab the treasure!'

'I'm not sure that's a good idea,' said Sheba. 'But we could have a little look, anyway.'

Remy started to unroll the paper tube, but instantly felt it crackle and split. He stopped, frightened that it might crumble to dust and leave them with nothing to exchange for his mother.

'I can't risk breaking it,' said Remy, looking up at Pyewacket, who was beginning to pout. 'I'm sorry.'

'We've got it, though!' Inji ruffled Remy's hair.

'Now all we have to do is find this Spider and offer to make a trade. The map for Sister Moon.'

'But how are we going to find them?' Remy asked. 'They could be anywhere in Paris.'

'I have a feeling they will find us firs—' Before she could finish her sentence – and as if to prove her right – there was a *swish* of something small and fast zipping through the air. It *plocked* into the side of Sheba's neck and stuck there: a tiny metal dart with a tuft of red feathers at the back. She raised a hand as if to pluck it out, fingers trembling, and then collapsed on the gravel floor, her skirts billowing around her.

'Sleeping dart!' Inji shouted. 'They're here!' She ripped off one of her leather gloves and just had time to bare her curved bone claws before a second dart hit her in the cheek. An instant later and she too was crumpling to the ground.

'Oh, flaming bobbins!' Pyewacket cried. He made to step in front of Remy but was shot as well. Right in the forehead, just above the rim of his goggles. His bulging, magnified eyes crossed as he tried to look up at the brightly coloured bloom of red. Then he let out a groan and toppled like a falling tree.

Remy knew he had less than a heartbeat before

more darts came flying from the shadows to knock him out like the others. So he did the only thing he could, the only thing he really knew how: he reached for the darkness that flowed all around him and gathered it in great clods, wrapping himself and the map up like bugs in a carpet. He stepped into the void, into the cold nothing. So deep and empty and hungry after lonely centuries down in the nethers of the city, it drank him in like a fine wine.

He vanished.

CHAPTER
TWELVE

In which Remy has to find a
way to rescue everybody.

Silence.

The red-tinted lantern dropped on the floor beside Sheba's limp hand, flickered and went out.

The darkness was complete. Not like a night sky, in which a scrap of starlight always managed to creep its way through even the thickest cloud. Not like the bowels of the ship he had stowed away on, in which flickering cinders from the stoked boilers sparked as the engines roared.

Down here, under countless feet of rock and

earth and history, there was an absence of all light. It could have been the bottom of the deepest sea, or the furthest corner of space.

Remy breathed it in, felt it coiled around himself like a suit of armour. Even though he should be terrified out of his wits right now, he was strangely calm. In one hand, he clutched the empty head of Pamplemousse. In the other, the brittle roll of paper that was Mama Rat's map.

And he waited.

*

Some time passed. It could have been minutes, it could have been years.

Eventually, a tiny sound came from outside the fountain room. A foot, shifting on the gritty floor.

Then there was a cough, the scrape of a match and the flash of a lantern being lit. Light flooded out, chasing away the frosty darkness that had been comforting Remy. Except he held on to wads of it, keeping himself hidden. A little chip of shadow beside the edge of the fountain bowl.

'Did we get 'em all?' The first voice to speak

sounded uncomfortably loud. It echoed off the walls with their coating of bones.

'All down,' said another. 'The Spider was right. They led us straight to the map.' This one spoke in English, but with a French accent.

'Couldn't we 'ave just waited for 'em to trade it to us?' The first voice again.

'Yes, but the boss wants the map *and* this bunch of oddments, though I'll be bludgered if I know why.'

'Who knows why the Spider does anything? We just follow orders.'

Remy recognised the voices from his memories of being tied and blindfolded in that cellar. And also his nightmares. The Spider's henchmen had found them.

But why didn't I hear their ticking? Remy wondered. *It should have been so loud down here. I should have heard them coming!*

As the four villains stepped into the circular room, Remy had his answer. They had tied layers and layers of rags around their mechanical limbs. All the grindings and ratchetings of their clockwork parts had been muffled and lost.

Two were women. One had dark brown skin, braided hair and a metal left hand with bladed fingers as big as kitchen knives. She clutched a gun with a long, thin barrel – the thing that had fired the darts. The other had oddly jointed legs covered by thick wrappings of knotted blankets, from which two spikes jutted, rather than feet. She balanced on them like a prowling insect. Her ice-blue eyes peered out from a pale face, almost hidden under a thatch of messy blonde hair.

The men followed them. The first was huge – almost as big as Gigantus – and had a steel claw instead of a right hand. In his left he held one of the bullseye lanterns from the entrance. A tattooed spiderweb crawled up his neck and across his bald head, blurring into the ruddy-pink skin of his face. His crooked nose was red and blotchy, full of broken veins from drinking too much wine.

Last into the room was a short, skinny fellow. He had dark olive skin, spiteful brown eyes and a ponytail of black hair. He wore a long greatcoat, spotted all over with grease and oil. The triple barrel of a gun poked from one of the sleeves, so long it almost scraped the floor.

They walked over to the sleeping bodies of his friends, poking and prodding them. From his pool of shadows behind the fountain, Remy held his breath.

'Where's the child?' said dagger-fingers. The others looked around the chamber.

'Must have scarpered,' said claw-hand. 'Gone off into the tunnels somewhere.'

'Well, I'm not looking for 'im.' Spider-legs glared at her comrades. 'I can't stand being cooped up down 'ere. Gives me the chills – all these ugsome bones everywhere.'

'I'll make sure to tell the Spider you said that, Bébé,' said rifle-arm. 'Now, which one has the map?'

Bébé crouched and gave Sheba a rough search. Then she scuttled over and did the same to Inji and Pyewacket. 'Not 'ere,' she said. 'That red-eyed brat must have taken it!'

'Batty-fangles and Chuzzlehumps!' the hulking claw-hand cursed.

'*Pas de problème.* I can track him.' Rifle-arm had a lantern of his own. He bent to light it, then moved to the chamber entrance, scanning the ground.

'What shall *we* do then?' claw-hand asked, his voice as thick as mince.

'Take them to the shop,' said rifle-arm. 'But don't go out the main entrance. It will attract too much attention.'

'How else are we supposed to leave?' claw-hand said. 'Burrow up through the mud?' His metal pincer clanked open and closed in anger.

'Ruby knows the way,' said rifle-arm. 'She used to live in the catacombs. Before *L'Araignée* found her.'

The woman with the dagger-fingers nodded. 'There was a whole gang of us. Pickpockets, burglars, muggers. I know lots of ways in and out. So happens there's an exit that shouldn't be too far from the shop. As long as the tunnels that way haven't flooded or fallen in – it's been a while since I've been down here.'

'Take them,' said rifle-arm, pointing at Sheba and the others with his gun-arm. 'But wait until dark before you leave. Their people might be looking for them.'

'You mean those freaks at the theatre?' Bébé said. 'They won't give us any trouble.'

'No, but they might call the Guard.' Ruby dagger-fingers bent down and got an arm underneath Inji's shoulders, heaving her up from the ground.

'*Bonne chance*,' said rifle-arm. And he disappeared from the doorway, heading deeper into the ossuary.

'That Pierre,' said the big man, his lip curled. 'Thinks he's cleverer than us all.'

'He's cleverer than *you*, Toby Tall,' said Bébé. 'But then again, so was the lump of black pudding I 'ad for breakfast. Now 'elp me with this gangling great-ape fellow, will you?'

The big man slung Sheba over one shoulder and then hefted Pyewacket up by the arm, sharing his weight with Bébé.

Thank goodness they can't see me, Remy thought. He tried to take the smallest, quietest breaths possible, watching from his shroud of shadows as his friends were hoisted from the floor. With Ruby carrying Inji, the villains began to lug the Carnival members out of the room, huffing, puffing and cursing as they went.

When they were gone, Remy took Pamplemousse from his pocket and carefully pushed the map inside the doll's empty head, easing it in through his missing eye. 'Guard this with your life,' he mouthed, not even daring to whisper. 'We have to follow them to this shop. It might be where they're keeping Mother.'

Pamplemousse stared up at him with his one

remaining eyeball. *And how do you plan on rescuing all of them on your own?* he seemed to say.

'I don't know yet,' said Remy, as silently as he could. 'But if we don't go with them, we'll be left in this place alone. With that gun-armed man hunting us.'

Pamplemousse didn't have an answer to *that*.

Praying that his shadow-camouflage held up, Remy tiptoed after the kidnappers and his still-sleeping friends.

*

If Remy had thought the skeleton-filled ossuary was the scariest part of the catacombs, he soon changed his mind.

Following the villains, he found himself leaving the bone-choked tourist attraction, and entering the old mines, where Parisians of the past had carved out all the limestone they could find.

Here, the tunnels were narrower, the ceilings lower. In some places, the walls had crumbled, leaving piles of rubble almost blocking the way. In others, water had pooled, sometimes as deep as his knees. And with him always was the constant fear that he might lose sight of Toby Tall and the others and be stuck, wandering in hopeless circles until he starved to death.

Although it would be hard to miss them, to be honest. The kidnappers struggled under the weight of his friends, moving at a painfully slow pace, moaning and bickering; edging their way sideways sometimes, metal limbs scraping sparks from the walls.

Remy kept as far back as he was able, well away from the circle of light cast by their lantern. He concentrated on every footstep, placing his booted feet as silently as possible. He waded through the puddles as slowly as a water snail, trying not to make the slightest splash. He kept his breathing slow and shallow, not wanting anything to give him away.

As they wound this way and that, past empty chambers and lumps of half-chiselled rock, he had plenty of time to worry. Mostly, he was afraid of the one called Pierre – the gun-armed man – coming up behind him to join his friends. He kept casting nervous glances back the way they had come, but there was no sign of him.

He also fretted about how he was going to rescue everybody. Besides being quite good at hiding, his Gifts hadn't given him any special powers. He couldn't fight like Inji or invent gadgets like Sheba. He couldn't read minds like Glyph or ... do whatever it was Pyewacket was good for.

There were his fangs, of course. But there was no way he would be able to creep up and bite *all* of the villains – and maybe the mysterious Spider too – without being seen. Then they would crush him like an insect. Besides which, his fangs weren't even poisonous. Not like his father's. The worst he could do would be to make them say 'ouch'.

Perhaps Methuselah could help? But he was as frail and weak as Remy. Verlaine hadn't seemed much stronger, and Lisette was an old woman. He couldn't even telegraph Glyph for aid, as the lines had been cut off.

Just wait and see, he told himself. *If you can at least find the address where they are holding Mother, that will be something.*

And so he kept following, just another silent shadow in the dark, lonely catacombs.

CHAPTER THIRTEEN

*In which Remy has to use his Gift
in ways he never imagined.*

At some point – it must have been at least an hour later, maybe more – the villains stopped and set Sheba and the others down. Bébé pulled some rope from her pack and began to tie the Carnival's hands behind their backs, while Ruby dagger-fingers scrambled up the side of the wall and disappeared through a hole in the ceiling, and Toby Tall searched them for weapons. Remy saw him take Sheba's clockwork pistol from her belt, and all the other items she had stashed in her dress pockets too.

Whatever they knocked them out with must be about to wear off, Remy realised. *That's why they're binding their hands. And this must be the exit. Ruby has gone up to check the coast is clear.* He found a crack in the wall and squeezed himself into it, keeping the darkness pulled tight around him. *I'll have to watch closely and follow them out as quickly as I can, so I don't lose them in the streets.*

He had no idea which part of Paris they were under. There could be rows of houses up there. They might even be outside the city walls, for all he knew. If he had come this far only to lose track of them in the space of time it took him to scramble out of the hole . . . he didn't know what he would do.

There was a patter of earth falling from the ceiling, and Ruby's head appeared, upside down.

'We're about two minutes' walk from the shop,' she said. 'But it's only five o'clock. The streets are still busy. What's the plan?'

Bébé gave Toby Tall a nervous look. 'We should do what Pierre says, I reckon. Wait here until it's dark, then hook it back, unseen-like.'

Toby grunted. 'Well, if I'm waiting here for three hours, I want some wine and food.' He took a handful of coins from his pocket and held them up to Ruby. 'Go and get us some drink and grub, will ya?'

Ruby cursed at him and spat, but took the money and disappeared with it, anyway.

Great, Remy thought. *Now I have to sit here and watch them eat. For hours.*

*

The worst thing about the wait was trying not to let his tummy rumble. That, and having to watch Toby Tall rip his way through a boiled ham and several baguettes of bread, chomping and burping like a wild animal.

Once or twice he saw one of his friends stir a little. A blink, or twitch of a hand. The drug from the darts was beginning to fade. If they woke up, might there be a chance they could free themselves? Could they fight off those three thugs without him having to perform a rescue?

He didn't get the chance to find out. Finally, eight o'clock rolled around, and Ruby went to look out the tunnel hole again.

'Sun's going down. It's close enough to dark, I reckon. Okay. Let's move them.'

Working quickly, Bébé climbed up out of the hole to join Ruby. The pair of them reached down and Toby Tall began to pass Sheba, Inji and Pyewacket up, one by one. In a few moments, they were all gone and the big man clambered up after them, using his claw to crunch hold of the rock wall as he went.

Quickly now, Remy told himself. *But carefully.*

He dashed out of his hiding place to the wall and began to climb. His little fingers gripped nubbins of jagged rock as he pulled himself up, but more than once he slipped. He tore a nail and scraped his leg badly, ripping his trousers at the knee. Finally, he slapped one hand on the outside of the tunnel entrance, and managed to haul himself out, arms burning from the effort. *Mother would be disappointed with me*, he thought. *She would have bounced out of there in one leap.*

But there wasn't time to worry about that. He had a quick look around and saw that he had emerged under a bush in the corner of an enormous graveyard. A tall stone wall surrounded the place: gravestones as far as the eye could see. And there, just leaving through a gate, were the kidnappers, with his friends being dragged along behind them.

Remy picked himself up and began to run after them. The instant he left the shade of the wall, he felt the heat of the sun on his skin. It was setting now, almost night, but there was an orange tinge to the sky and enough light to make his face burn. His mask was still stuffed in his coat pocket, but there was no time to pull it on. Gritting his teeth, he tore through the cemetery and out of the gate, skidding to a halt in the street beyond.

It was a wide boulevard that would once have been lined with trees but, like the roads he had seen yesterday, they had all been hacked down to use for barricades. In the distance he could see the villains, walking alongside the cemetery wall, hugging the shadows. Remy did the same, welcoming the escape from the last rays of the sun. He draped himself in as much evening gloom as he could – there were only a few people out on the streets now, but the last thing he wanted was for one of them to spot him and scream something stupid about a vampire. He would end up being captured, like his friends.

Trotting along, he soon caught up with his quarry, and then hung back sixty feet or so. Just enough to see where they were going. They trudged along, crossed the next street, and then turned left down a road that seemed to be lined with cafés and theatres. Rue de la Gaîté, Remy read on a street sign.

Most of the restaurants seemed to be closed for the night, shutters down and doors locked. A few small groups of National Guard walked by, but they were too busy laughing and talking to each other to notice either the kidnappers or Remy. The shadows were darker here, at least, and his skin stopped its painful itching and burning. He clung to shop doorways and gloomy corners, inching his way along, letting the shade cool his face.

About halfway down the street, the kidnappers stopped next to a narrow building. One of them opened the door with a key, and then they all went inside.

Still sixty feet behind them, Remy reached the building just as the front door banged shut. He heard the loud *clunk* of the lock turning and a bolt being shot home. To his horror, he realised there was no way to follow them, at least not through the front door.

What shall I do? he panicked. If he had been Sheba, he could have picked the lock. Inji or

Pyewacket, and he could have climbed up the building and found a way in through a window.

But he was just pathetic, timid Remiel. The only thing he was good for was hiding himself away.

He hovered outside the locked door, trying to come up with some kind of plan. Then he realised he was standing out in plain sight. Probably not a good idea.

Scurrying across the street, Remy found a shady doorway and crouched inside, drawing the shadows good and tight. From here, he had a better view of the building his friends had been taken into: it was a shabby old clothes shop, with peeling paint on the wooden shutters that hid the windows. Posters had been pasted over them – mostly adverts for a *'Parapluie Réductible de Poche',* a folding pocket umbrella – suggesting that the place had been closed for quite some time.

He looked up, noting the building had four storeys, and windows in the steeply sloping roof. The Carnival could be in any one of those rooms. His mother too. If only there was a way to get inside!

Not knowing what to do, Remy took Pamplemousse from his pocket to ask him. The little china head looked ridiculous with the roll of yellowed paper jutting out of one eye.

The map, he thought. *I still have it. Maybe I should knock on the door and offer it to them, in return for Mother and my friends?*

No, that was a stupid idea. They would just grab him, and then *everyone* would be captive, and the map gone. Perhaps his best bet would be to remember the address, then find his way back across the city to ask Methuselah for help. It was a long way to go, but at least it was dark now. Or was it? The sky above flashed bright with a sudden flare, followed by a low, rumbling boom.

Thunder? But it had been clear and sunny all day. And then the penny dropped, as he realised what it was: explosions. The Prussian guns had started firing on the city.

Remy crouched smaller in the doorway. He looked up at the rooftops and chimney pots, expecting to see cannonballs screaming out of the sky, smashing them into exploding clouds of fire and slate.

None came. The rumbling just continued, the sky lit up every now and then with blazes of orange and red.

On and on it went. Remy even saw some guardsmen walk past, laughing about it.

'The Prussians only have their small guns,' one said. 'It will be a different story when they bring up their cannons. But our armies will have charged in from the country by then. We'll storm out of the walls and crush them between us.'

'Still, I wouldn't want to be living in Vaugirard,' said another. 'I bet it's raining hot lead.'

They ambled past Remy's doorway, chatting, laughing and sharing slurps from a wine bottle, not ever knowing he was there.

'If I was a soldier at war, I'd be a lot more worried about everything,' he whispered to Pamplemousse. 'What if we went and told them our friends had been kidnapped? Do you think they would help?'

Pamplemousse just stared, in a way that said *don't be ridiculous.*

Remy sighed. The doll's head was right. The guardsmen, half drunk, would just stand and laugh at him. Probably, they would call some of their friends over. Then there would be a whole crowd of them, shouting and jeering, attracting attention and alerting the kidnappers to his presence.

'This is *impossible*.' Remy felt like crying. To be so close to his mother, yet unable to help . . .

There was another flash in the sky, lighting up the street with blinking light. And there, caught in the jittering glare as he stormed along the pavement, was Pierre rifle-arm. The man was clearly furious at returning from the catacombs empty-handed. He stamped his boots hard enough to crack the cobbles, he glowered and frowned like he'd just chewed on a lemon, and the long barrel of his gun-arm swung back and forth as he marched.

This is my chance, thought Remy. He knew the door would have to be unlocked to let Pierre into the shop – if Remy could get close enough to slip in as well . . . But that would mean creeping right behind his own hunter. He had never tried to use his hiding skill so near to someone. Would he be discovered? Was it worth the risk?

There wasn't time to think it through carefully. Pierre's marching pace had brought him to the shop doorway already, and he was raising his fist to pound on the door. Remy sucked in a deep breath, summoned as much shade as he could, and ran across the street.

*

Boom! Boom! Boom!

Pierre's clenched fist bashed against the splintered wood, making a noise louder than the distant Prussian guns.

'*Mon dieu!*' he shouted. 'Open up at once!'

Remy, hoping the man's rage would make him careless, scampered right behind him, crouching just by his feet. Pierre's long coat would hide Remy from whoever opened the door, but if he stepped back or, worse, looked behind him, then it was all over.

Please don't turn around. Remy thought the words over and over in his head, as if they were a spell that might keep him safe. He heard heavy footsteps on the other side of the door, the scrape of the bolt, the click of the lock . . .

'Hurry it up!' Pierre shouted again, making Remy jump.

'All right, all right.' It was Toby Tall on the other side, creaking the door slowly open. 'Keep your *pantalettes* on.'

Pierre raised his gun-arm and shoved at the door, forcing his way inside with a snarl.

This is my chance, Remy realised. *I have to get inside before Toby shuts the door. And all without being seen.*

Keeping close to the ground, Remy moved as if he was stuck to Pierre's heels, no more than an inch from the swishing hem of his long coat. He focused on squeezing the darkness around him, straining so hard that his head hurt. It felt like his eyeballs might pop, and his heart was beating so loud, he was sure they would be able to hear it.

Step. Step. Pierre moved inside the shop, squeezing through the gap between door and frame. Remy moved with him, almost stumbling over the doorstep, face brushing against the leather coat. It stank of gun-oil and grease.

'Steady on.' Toby Tall's voice came from somewhere above him. As soon as Pierre was inside the shop, the huge man began to close the door. Remy felt the air move as it passed his face, the edge of it brush his leg and then ... *clonk*! His trailing heel was trapped and pinched in the door frame.

Remy bit his lip to try and stop yelping, but his two sharp fangs popped into his skin, hurting even more. Toby Tall made a puzzled noise, wondering why the door hadn't closed. He opened it again, allowing Remy to jerk his foot free, sending him half tumbling into the shop, almost sprawling on the floor.

Had the room beyond been bare and empty or, even worse, brightly lit by gas lamps, then he would have been spotted instantly. Luckily – oh, so luckily – every scrap of space on the shop floor was filled with racks of old coats, capes and jackets. Boxes and tumbled piles of cobweb-laced shoes and dresses spilling into one another. There were no lights, and thick, gloopy shadows were everywhere. Black ones, purple ones, all choked with dust and threads and mildew.

As soon as Remy entered the shop, he could feel them. He was already concentrating on cloaking himself so completely, the new shadows rushed over him like waves crashing on a beach. If any part of him had indeed been visible, it vanished in a heartbeat under a tide of gathered darkness.

'Stupid old building,' Toby Tall muttered behind him, giving the door a good slam. He turned the key in the lock and rammed the bolt across.

Remy had done it. He was inside.

CHAPTER FOURTEEN

In which the Carnival meet an old friend.

Huddled under a rack of coats, Remy finally allowed himself to breathe.

He couldn't quite believe it, but there was no time to celebrate. He still had four mechanical-limbed villains to somehow defeat and four adults to rescue. Keeping himself as small and quiet as possible, he began to inch through the shadows.

After locking the door, Toby Tall had stomped past him, through the shop towards a room at the back. Voices could be heard coming from there now: the loudest of which belonged to Pierre rifle-arm.

'I searched the *entire* place!' he yelled. 'There was no sign of the little brat!'

'Well, where else could 'e have gone?' That sounded like Bébé.

'Who knows?' Pierre again. 'All I can tell you is that he wasn't in the ossuary. I looked inside every pile of bones, every mound of skulls. You idiots let him slip past you somehow!'

'You're just as much of an idiot as us,' said Toby Tall. 'In fact, you were the one who told us to leave so you could find him. I think you should go and explain all this to the Spider.'

'We'll *all* go,' said Pierre. 'I'm not taking the blame for this myself.'

'But what about the captives?' Ruby spoke up. 'Someone has to stay and watch them.'

'I'll do that,' said Toby. 'I'm chuzzled out after lugging them all the way back here.'

'Fine,' said Pierre. 'At least we have got this "Carnival". It will give her something to be pleased about.'

'Don't be so sure,' said Ruby. Footsteps sounded and, from where Remy was hidden under a collection of lace petticoats, he saw three sets of boots pass by. Or rather, two sets of boots and a pair of steel spikes.

So the Spider is a woman, he half thought. But his mind was more focused on the villains. That, and who might be in the other room with his trussed-up friends. He waited until the feet had gone by and the shop door had closed behind them. Then he waited some more, as the heavy tread of Toby Tall stomped its way up what sounded like a staircase.

Finally, when he was certain that all four of them had gone, Remy crept from his hiding place and inched towards the back room.

Weaving between the mounds of dusty clothing, the rickety coat racks and faceless felt mannequins, he could feel his hands begin to tremble. *What if Mother isn't there?* he thought. *What if they are keeping her somewhere else? What if they've killed her?*

He hardly dared think the last thought, but a dark part of him knew it was possible.

By the time he reached the doorway at the rear of the shop front, his whole body was shaking, and tears had begun to prickle the corner of his eyes.

Through the door was another room, this

one lit by a small oil lamp on a shelf. In the dim orange light, he could see more piles of clothing, a dressmaker's table, rolls of thread, sheets of paper patterns. There were four chairs in the room, each one holding a slumped figure, bound and gagged. Remy recognised Pyewacket, Inji, Sheba and another ... a woman dressed in filthy grey trousers and a once-white shirt, ripped and torn at the seams. Her head hung down, her face covered by a mop of matted black hair. As Remy's foot scuffed the dusty floor, she looked up ...

A gag covered her mouth, and there were fresh bruises on her cheek and forehead. Dried blood caked one nostril, but Remy couldn't mistake those eyes: pure, glinting orbs of black, like two chips of polished jet.

'Mother!' he whispered the name as loudly as he dared, and rushed to her, leaping into her lap and wrapping his arms around her neck as tightly as he could. He squeezed and squeezed, breathing in her smell, rubbing his face against her hair, never ever wanting to let go.

But he had to. He still wasn't safe. Toby Tall could burst into the room at any moment. Or the others might suddenly return, maybe even with the Spider ...

Reluctantly, he let his mother go and reached up to pull the gag down from her mouth.

'I did it, Mother,' he whispered. 'I found the Carnival. And Marie's map.'

'Oh, my wonderful, wonderful boy,' she whispered back, tears spilling down her face. 'I didn't think I'd ever see you again.'

'I didn't think I'd see you either.' Remy wiped her cheeks with his sleeve. 'But I have to get you out quickly. Before they come back.'

His mother shook her head. 'They have me in handcuffs still. But the others are tied with rope. Go to Sheba. She'll have a way out, if I know her.'

Hopping down from his mother's lap, Remy turned to the Carnival, tied in their chairs. They were awake now, he saw. Sheba's eyes were gleaming orange, lit up by the lamp, or perhaps something smouldering inside. He tiptoed over to her and carefully pulled down the rag she had been gagged with.

'Remy,' she breathed. 'I don't think I've ever been so pleased to see somebody.'

'I hid when they shot you,' he explained. 'Then I followed them here. How do I get you out? They took all your weapons and gadgets.'

'Not all,' whispered Sheba. 'Go around behind me and pull up my shirt.'

'Your shirt?' Remy felt his cheeks burn bright red. 'I can't do that!'

'You have to,' said Sheba. 'Quickly now. Lift my shirt and look at my corset.'

Remy wasn't at all familiar with women's undergarments. His mother mostly wore men's clothes – certainly nothing like a corset. But he knew that it was fashionable for ladies to squeeze in their waists with laced-up supports; the smaller and thinner the better.

Still blushing, he pulled up Sheba's shirt until he could see the corset underneath. It ran around her body from the waist to just below her shoulder blades, was tied together with a long row of laces down the back and had vertical supports spaced around it. It looked like the least comfortable thing in the world to wear.

'Now,' said Sheba, 'next to the laces, the first stay on the left. Pull it out.'

Remy remembered reading that the upright struts around the corset were called 'stays' and that they were usually made of whalebone. Not knowing what good a piece of whale would do in this situation, he pinched hold of the top of it and pulled, trying hard not to accidentally touch the bare skin of Sheba's shoulders.

Out slid the stay, and he was surprised to see it wasn't bone at all, but a very long, thin knife with a delicate ivory handle.

'Be careful,' Sheba whispered. 'It's very sharp. You can use it to cut my ropes.'

Remy grasped the knife handle and knelt to where Sheba's hands were tied. The blade sliced right through the cord like it was butter. As Sheba rubbed her sore wrists, Remy moved on to her ankles and cut the rope there too.

'Well done.' Sheba smiled at him. Remy took Pamplemousse from his pocket and held him up, the rolled-up map still poking from his eye.

'I've got the map,' he said. 'Do you want it? Or shall we just tear it up?'

'I think it should stay where it is for now, don't you?' Sheba said, smiling. 'Pamplemousse seems to be doing a very good job of looking after it. Now, why don't you free the others, while I set about unlocking your mother?'

'She's handcuffed,' Remy said. 'And we don't know where the key is.'

'That's never stopped me before.' Sheba reached up to her hair and pulled out some pins, then she moved swiftly across the room to her old friend Sister Moon.

Not wasting any time, Remy dashed over to Inji and cut her loose. She thanked him with a quick hug and a peck on the cheek. Blushing even more, he went to set Pyewacket free. The poor fellow had a big red pockmark in the centre of his forehead where the dart had struck him.

'Brilliant work, my lad,' he whispered, as Remy undid his gag and started cutting him loose. 'Of course, I planned for us to get captured all along. You played your part perfectly, as I deduced you would.'

Chuckling, Remy turned, just in time to see Sheba unlock his mother's handcuffs. He ran to her again, and this time she hugged him back.

'Brave boy,' she whispered in his ear. 'Brave, clever boy.'

Remy was so happy, he thought he might explode.

'You should be very proud of him,' said Sheba. 'He has been so brave, so desperate to find you.'

Sister Moon reached up to take Sheba's hand. 'Thank you for coming,' she said, beginning to cry again. 'I had no right to put you all in danger, but thank you.'

Sheba bent down and wrapped her arms around Moon and Remy both. 'You had every right. We're your family – you've no idea how much we've missed you. All those years . . .'

'I'm sorry,' Sister Moon sobbed. 'I wanted to come to you. I needed to, but . . . I didn't dare take Remy out of Paris. But I couldn't. Not after what happened . . .'

'We know,' said Sheba. 'We met Methuselah and he told us everything. If only I could have been there for you . . .'

'I heard too, Mama,' said Remy. 'You should have told me before. Papa was so brave, wasn't he?'

Sister Moon choked back another sob. 'He was. Just like you. I'm sorry, Remy. I wanted to tell you, but every time I tried . . .'

They wrapped their arms about each other, tears

streaming down their faces. Sheba held them both, then Pyewacket was there as well, hugging and weeping.

'This is Inji,' Sheba said, in between sobs. 'She's part of our family now too.'

'Get in here, cat-features,' said Pyewacket. He grabbed Inji with one of his long arms and pulled her into the huddle.

For a long time, they held each other – all the explanations, all the apologies, all the words that hadn't been said over the twenty missing years – none of it was needed. And, snuggled in the middle of everyone, like a rabbit in his burrow, Remy felt as warm and safe as he ever had in his life.

'What the chumbly flibbins is this?' a voice boomed, echoing around the shabby room. Peeping through a gap in the arms around him, Remy could see Toby Tall, standing in the side doorway, a look of violent shock on his face.

Instantly, the Carnival members – past and present – flew apart, leaping to face the claw-armed brute. Remy tumbled to the floor, but Pyewacket scooped him up and hooked him clear of danger.

'Best we stay out of this one, me old chum,' he

said, moving them both to the side of the room. From his arms, Remy could see Inji popping her claws, baring her teeth, the fur on her face and ears bristling. His mother rose from her chair, flexing her stiff limbs, a look of murderous fury on her face. And Sheba . . . he finally saw what made her a part of the Carnival, what marked her as Gifted like the rest of them. Hair had begun to sprout from her smooth, porcelain skin. Her nose was stretching, melting into a wolf's muzzle, complete with gleaming, hungry fangs; and her eyes – blazing amber – were two points of deadly fire in her snarling, feral face.

'You dollymops don't know who you're messing with,' said Toby. He hefted his pincer arm, making it clack and clank, open and shut.

'Oh, *you* don't know who you're messing with,' said Inji. She was actually grinning, her needle-sharp teeth glinting in the lamplight.

Sister Moon, Remy's mother, reached down and picked up the narrow corset-knife from the floor. With a flick of her wrist, she sent it zipping across the room, smashing through the thin glass of the lamp and slicing the flame from the wick. The place was plunged into complete darkness.

As if that was a signal, the three women moved as one, surging towards the towering figure of Toby Tall, who was flailing around blindly in the darkness.

Remy, of course, could see everything clearly with his crimson vision. He saw the streaks of glowing fire that were Sheba's eyes. They streamed across the room as she ran on all fours, leaping up to Toby's face with a snarl.

He saw Inji duck and roll, dodging the metal claw, springing up on to Toby's back and slicing at the harness that held his clockwork arm in position.

And he almost saw his mother – except she moved too quickly to pin down. One blink and she was across the room, another and she was kicking Toby Tall in his stomach, his shins, his neck. Then she was gone again, punching and striking him from the other side.

'What's going on?' Pyewacket said beside him. 'I can't see a blooming thing!'

But there was no time for Remy to explain. Before he could even open his mouth, Toby Tall collapsed to the ground with a floorboard-splintering crash. His mechanical arm fell away, the cogs and tubes and joints all bent, sliced and mangled. There was a final clicking sound as Sister Moon jumped across the room, grabbed the handcuffs that had been used to bind her and fastened them on to the big man's legs, and then Inji struck a match and lit the broken lamp again. The battleground appeared, and Pyewacket could see Toby: bound and unconscious, with hundreds of tooth and claw marks lacing his head and shoulders.

'Well,' he said to Remy. 'I was about to step in and help, but they seem to have handled it nicely.'

Sheba was crouched on the floor, breathing heavily. Remy could see her nose returning to its normal button shape, the fur shrinking into her skin. But her eyes – they still blazed, deep inside the pupils. 'We should go,' she said, a slight trace of growl in her voice. 'The others will be back soon.'

'Wait,' said Sister Moon. 'I think they have other hostages here. I've heard them . . . upstairs.'

Inji looked to the side door, where Toby had come from. A stairway could be seen, leading to a murky upper floor. She wrinkled her nose and sniffed. 'I can smell two people,' she said. 'But we'd better be quick. I'm still dozy from that drugged dart – I'm not fighting as well as I should.'

'You just took down a brute the size of a giant elephant,' said Pyewacket. 'I think you three could beat the entire Prussian army.'

'Let's hope we don't have to,' said Sister Moon, and she took Remy by the hand, leading him up the stairs.

*

At the top of the steps was a small landing, its walls bare apart from large cracks in the plaster. Walking across, they found themselves in a spacious room that would have looked out over the Rue de la Gaîté, if the windows hadn't been covered with blankets and scraps of old clothing.

Flickering gaslights cast wavy shadows across the faded wallpaper. There was an upturned chair in the corner, next to a table that held the remains of Toby Tall's second dinner. Sheba's weapons and Pyewacket's goggles were spread among the breadcrumbs and dirty plates, but the thing that drew Remy's eye was a large metal cage pushed up against the wall. Crumpled in the corner, nestling in a drift of paper scraps, was the figure of an elderly lady. She wore heavily patched and frayed skirts, a battered leather waistcoat, and had a mad jumble of white curly hair that frothed and spiralled all over her head in corkscrew tangles. There were pencil stubs and screwdrivers poking out all over it, as if she had put them there for safekeeping and then forgotten they existed. When Remy and the others entered the room, she looked up at them through steel-rimmed spectacles so thick that her eyes swam around in them like giant grey goldfish in bowls.

'Ratchets,' she said, squinting at them. Her voice cracked and reedy. 'Spokes. Camshafts. Handcranks.'

Remy was about to ask his mother what she was talking about, when he heard both her and Sheba gasp at the same time.

'By Wellington's overgrown nose hair!' Pyewacket shouted. 'It can't be? Can it?'

'Axle grease,' said the old woman. 'Flywheels.' She turned away from them and started scribbling on a piece of crumpled paper with a chewed pencil stub.

'It is,' said Sheba, walking to the cage bars. 'It has to be.'

'What are you all talking about?' Inji asked. She looked as confused as Remy.

'This woman,' said Sister Moon. 'We knew her. Back in London. She built a machine that was stealing children from the banks of the River Thames.'

'But we stopped her and then Gigantus stuck her in a monkey cage,' said Pyewacket. 'Do you think she's been there all this time?'

Sheba bent down by the cage. 'Spindlecrank?' she said. 'Belinda? Do you remember us? Can you tell us who put you in this cage? Was it someone you worked for once?'

'Surely you don't think it was *her*?' Sister Moon said. 'Not Mrs Crowley?'

'What?' Pyewacket shouted, far too loudly. 'The woman who ordered the mudlarks to be stolen and nearly blew us up at the Great Exhibition? But she's dead! I pushed her into a flaming pit of fire myself!'

'It would explain how the Spider knew Mama Rat and Sister Moon were connected,' said Sheba. She went over to the table and retrieved her little pistol, holding it up for Spindlecrank to see. Remy could see a slight tremble in her hand as she raised it. Clearly, the mention of this Crowley woman had shaken her. Brought back terrible memories, maybe. 'What about this, Belinda? Does it ring any bells?'

The woman looked up and seemed to notice them for the first time. She shot across to the bars and reached out for the pistol. Her long, knobbled fingers ran over it, tracing the clockwork key and its ring of little barrels. 'My pistol!' she said. 'I've been looking for it for so long! Pivots! Hinges! Springs!'

Sheba gently took it back. 'Can you tell us how you got here, Belinda? Were you taken from London? How long have you been held prisoner?'

'I'm afraid you'll find her mind has quite gone.' A voice came from the far corner of the room, making them all jump. They had forgotten about the second hostage.

Remy peered around his mother's legs to see a bruised and battered man with a white beard and balding head. He lay among a tumble of dirty blankets, handcuffed to a gas pipe in the wall. One of his eyes was swollen shut, and there was dried blood all over his smart shirt.

'Who are you?' Sheba said. 'And what do you know of Spindlecrank?'

The old man struggled to sit up, his cuffed hand clanking against the pipe. 'My name is D'Aramon,' he said. He spoke English well, but with the hint of a French accent. 'She was here when they captured me, several months ago. But she was taken from Paris, not London. She often talks of a workshop she had, in the third arrondissement.'

'D'Aramon!' Remy remembered the name. 'You were the one who got Mama Rat put in prison!'

'She's a good friend of ours,' said Inji. Her claws were still visible. She tensed them, making her knuckles pop.

The man hung his head. 'That was a long time ago,' he said. 'And – if it is worth anything – I am very sorry for it. For many years I have been just a simple businessman. I am ashamed of how I once behaved . . . and now I am ashamed again for telling these villains about Marie's map. I never thought I would be one to break under torture . . . But I did, in the end. Have they harmed her?'

'She's safe,' said Sheba. 'Well hidden. And we would like her to remain so.'

'She's in no danger from me, I promise,' said D'Aramon. 'Even if she was, I fear those brutes have broken something inside of me. I don't suppose I shall live much longer.'

'We can get you to a doctor,' said Sheba. 'And Spindlecrank as well.' She took another hairpin from her head and began to pick the lock on his handcuffs.

'Thank you.' D'Aramon wiped a tear from his eye. 'I don't deserve such mercy. If there's anything I can do to help, just ask.'

'What do you know about the Spider?' Sister Moon asked. 'Anything you might have overheard may be useful.'

His wrist free, D'Aramon struggled to stand up. Pyewacket helped to support him. 'Her henchmen kidnapped me as I was walking home from my offices one evening. They knew I had once worked as a spymaster, and they wanted me to spill all the precious secrets I had hoarded from those long-ago years. I held out for as long as I could, but in the end ... I told them everything. Including what I knew about Marie and her map. Once they had reported *that* to their boss ... well, they weren't interested in anything else.'

'Did you ever meet the Spider?' Remy asked. 'I know she's a woman, but that's all.'

D'Aramon shook his head. 'No,' he said. 'Her gang locked me up with Belinda here. The poor woman has been kept prisoner for over a decade building the machines that turned the Spider's henchmen into monsters. They call her "the Mechanic". I believe, on that desk there, is her notebook of designs. They recently had her working on some new kind of secret weapon. You may discover some useful information inside.'

Remy ran to the table and found a small, leather-bound book. He flicked through it, seeing pages filled with sketches and inventions. Among them were contraptions that looked like Toby Tall's claw, Bébé's spider legs and others. He handed the book to Sheba.

'Thank you,' she said. 'This will prove handy, I'm sure.'

Tucking the book into one of her many hidden pockets, Sheba pulled out some more hairpins. Within seconds, she had picked the lock of Spindlecrank's cage and was helping the old woman shuffle out of it.

'Belinda, what was the weapon you built?' Sister Moon asked her. 'Can you remember why they wanted it?'

'Gears. Handbrakes. Combustion. Kiss. Kiss,' she muttered away to herself, lost again in her strange, mechanical world.

'Well, we're not getting anything out of *her*,' said Inji. 'We should get someone to look at her, as soon as possible.'

'But she might know who the Spider is!' Pyewacket protested. 'Can't we question her some more? What if it *is* Mrs Crowley? That woman is evil!'

'There's no time,' said Sheba. 'The gang could be back at any minute, and poor Belinda is in no state to answer anything. I don't want her to suffer any more. Besides, you were right. Crowley is long dead. There must be some other link.'

'Let's find one of those hotels that have become hospitals,' said Inji. 'They will have medics and nurses to care for these two.'

'What about Toby lard-brain downstairs?' Pyewacket said. 'We can't just leave him there. What if someone comes along and lets him go?'

'I may be able to help with that,' said D'Aramon. 'I still have a few friends in high places from my government days. I shall happily have him arrested, and word put out to stop the others.'

'And do you promise you'll leave Mama Rat alone?' Remy asked, looking up at him.

'You have saved my life,' said D'Aramon. 'And treated me better than I could have hoped. You have my solemn vow.'

Remy wasn't entirely sure he trusted him, but a promise was better than nothing. With the two freed hostages limping between them, the Carnival made their way out of the old clothes shop and into the dark streets beyond.

CHAPTER FIFTEEN

*In which the Carnival are
hunted through Paris.*

I t didn't take them long to find one of the
converted war hospitals, this time in a theatre
on the same road as the Spider's base. They left
D'Aramon and Spindlecrank with a confused but
helpful nurse, and then hurried away from Rue de la
Gaîté as quickly as possible.

With Sister Moon leading them, they walked
briskly through the Paris streets, keeping off the
main boulevards and avoiding marching patrols of
National Guard. They crossed the Seine over the
Pont des Invalides, passed some grand palaces and

ornate buildings, and then lost themselves in a maze of side streets and alleys.

Finally, they entered a run-down apartment building and walked up several flights of stairs to the top floor. To Remy's surprise, his mother had a key.

'What's this place?' he said, as they walked into a small, sparsely furnished attic apartment. A single window looked out from the living room over the night-time rooftops to the cloudy sky above, which still flashed every now and then with flames of cannon fire.

Sister Moon gave him a sheepish look. 'It's a place I kept. For my work, mostly. And in case we ever needed somewhere safe to run to. I'm afraid there's no food, but I have some money and clothes stashed away.'

'Why didn't you tell me about it?' Remy asked. He was afraid his mother wasn't the person he thought he knew at all. There seemed to be secrets upon secrets, making him wonder what else was being hidden from him.

'I'm sorry, Remy,' she said. 'There was no need to tell you. I used to leave, come here to get changed and then do my work.'

'Hmm,' said Pyewacket, rubbing his chin. 'A secret hideaway, night work, "need-to-know" ... I deduce that you were a master criminal! No? Jewel thief? Assassin? Spy?'

'Nothing so glamorous,' said Sister Moon. 'I used to deliver packages. Although they were secret ones, and for some quite unpleasant people. I'm not proud of it, but I had to put food on our plates somehow.'

'Nobody is judging you,' said Sheba. 'Although I wish we had known what you were going through. We'd have been on the next boat across the Channel.'

Sister Moon blinked back tears again. But enough of those had been shed for one night. 'If you don't mind.' She tugged at her ruined shirt and ragged trousers. 'I think I will get changed. Make yourselves at home.'

And she disappeared into the bedroom, leaving the others to collapse on the few rickety chairs in exhaustion.

*

Remy fell asleep almost as soon as he sat down. He awoke in the apartment's bedroom, thin rays of sunlight trickling in through the shutters to pool on the floorboards (luckily, a safe distance from where he lay). At some point, his mother must have carried him in here, taken off his jacket and boots, and tucked him in for the night.

With a yawn and a joint-popping stretch, he sat up and looked around. Pamplemousse sat on the bedside table, quietly watching him. Mama Rat's map still poked out from his eye.

'We did it,' Remy said to him. 'We rescued Mother. And we didn't even need to trade the map to do it.'

Pamplemousse stared. Motes of dust drifted around him, glowing in the beams of light.

'I wonder what time it is,' Remy said. 'I feel like I slept for weeks. I was *so* tired.'

Pulling on his jacket and boots, he tucked Pamplemousse into his pocket and walked through to the other room. It was full of the smell of bacon, freshly baked bread and coffee.

'Good morning, darling,' said his mother. She was standing by the stove, frying breakfast in a heavy iron pan. Remy noticed she had changed into a shirt and trousers of midnight black. She had a new pair of smoked-glass spectacles on, hiding her ebony eyes, and she was wearing her leather knife belt. Although both sheaths were empty. The Spider's henchman must have taken her blades when she was captured.

'Did you sleep well?' Inji asked. She was sitting upright in a nest of blankets on the floor, a cup of steaming coffee clutched in her hands.

'Yes, thank you,' said Remy. 'What time is it?'

'Nearly midday,' said Sheba. She was in the apartment's only armchair, Spindlecrank's notebook on her lap. Pyewacket lay on a heap of cushions beside her, snoring away.

'So late!' Remy said. 'Do you think D'Aramon's friends will have arrested the Spider yet? Is it safe to go back to our home now? Can Sheba and Inji come and stay with us too?'

'Too many questions!' Sister Moon laughed. She served him up a plate of bacon and some slices of fresh bread. 'Eat first, and then we will plan the future.'

Remy realised he hadn't had any food since yesterday morning. He was starving. Using his fingers, he began to shovel the strips of greasy bacon into his mouth, wiping the dribbling juices off his chin with hunks of crusty loaf.

'Slow down,' said Sheba, laughing. 'You'll give yourself indigestion!'

'Sorry,' said Remy, stifling a burp.

'I think we should talk about what our next steps are, though,' Sheba said, once everyone had finished eating. 'Unfortunately, we can't count on the Spider and her remaining friends to be caught. We must assume they are still looking for us.'

'I was very careful when I went shopping,' said Sister Moon. 'But I didn't spot any sign of them.'

'They're still out there,' said Inji. 'I can feel it in my fur.'

'In that case,' said Sheba, 'it won't be safe for you to return to your apartment. Not yet. The Spider will still be after the map.'

'I heard them say she wanted you, as well,' said Remy, thinking back to that horrible moment in the catacombs. Hiding behind the fountain and listening to the villains talk.

'You did?' Sheba tugged at a loose lock of hair. 'What could she want *us* for?'

'We're witnesses, aren't we?' said Inji. 'We know

about the map and them kidnapping Sister Moon and Remy. We're a loose end that needs tying up.'

'Yes,' said Sheba. 'Someone who weaves as carefully as the Spider would hate us. We could find ourselves being victims of this secret weapon she had Spindlecrank build her.'

'Are there any clues to what is was?' Remy asked. 'In her book, perhaps?' He peered over at the sketches, fascinated by the intricate patterns of cogs and wheels.

'There are notes for all the artificial limbs she has made for the Spider's gang.' Sheba held up the book and flicked through the pages. 'But there's nothing about the weapon D'Aramon mentioned. Although several pages have been torn from the back, right under this unpleasant-sounding title: "The Spider's Kiss".'

'I'm sure Spindlecrank said something about a kiss,' said Remy. 'In among all those nonsense words she was babbling.'

'Yes, she did!' Inji beamed at him, 'Well remembered, Remy! Could the Kiss be the weapon?'

'It sounds likely,' said Sheba. 'But as to what form it might take ... I don't want to wait around and find out. We have to leave the city, as quickly as possible.'

Sister Moon frowned at this. 'That could be tricky. It depends on how much of the Prussian army is out there.'

'We can slip through easily though, can't we?' Remy imagined a daring night-time escape, sneaking through the lines of snoozing Prussian soldiers in the fields, and then a trip back to London – where there were still so many sights to see, so much to explore . . .

'Remy.' Sister Moon crouched beside him, giving him one of her serious looks. 'I don't mind helping the others to find a way out. But I think you and I should stay here. Where I can watch over you . . . keep you safe.'

'But Mother!' Remy couldn't believe what he was hearing. 'If we stay here, the Spider will find us and capture us again! The Carnival can look after me. And if you are there too, that's the safest I can possibly be!' He suddenly knew, as much as he loved his mother, he didn't want to lose this new thing; this feeling of *belonging* somewhere. He wanted to stay with the Carnival, even if it meant leaving Paris.

'We will talk about it later,' said Sister Moon, just as Pyewacket sat up and yawned.

'What's all the shouting about?' he said, peering blearily around the room. 'Can't you see some of us are trying to sleep?'

'Something else you may not like,' said Sheba, as Pyewacket began his morning routine of scratching all the various nooks and crannies of his body. 'We left our luggage and equipment with Methuselah at the Théâtre de Rêves. We should return and collect it. Of course, you don't have to come with us, if it's too painful . . .'

Sister Moon was silent. She began to collect the plates, her mouth set in a grim line, until Remy reached up and took her hand. 'Please, Mother,' he said. 'Methuselah and the others care for you very much. I think it will be good for you to see them.'

'Very well.' She almost whispered it, and then bustled off to the sink with an armful of plates.

*

They waited until nightfall, until the shadows of the gas-lit streets gave them some cover from spying eyes.

The Prussian bombardment had started again,

less enthusiastically than the first night, but with enough distant booms and flashes to make Remy nervous. He was already on edge, listening out for the *tickticktick* of clockwork engines, looking for the sly face of Pierre rifle-arm, or the oddly jointed legs of Bébé; expecting one of them to leap out of every doorway and alley entrance that they passed.

There were crowds of people out in the streets tonight, cheering whenever a squad of guardsmen marched past. They seemed to be expecting them to charge out and attack the Prussians but, as far as Remy could see, they were walking around aimlessly. Nobody was getting ready to charge anywhere.

And always, they heard the relentless booming of the bombardment. It didn't seem to be doing much damage, even as they neared the northern edge of the city. At least, not until they reached the Théâtre itself.

The entire top floor of the building was missing, ragged chunks of the wall blown away, and burnt timbers sticking up like broken teeth. Trails of black smoke still rose from the wreckage, and there was a crowd of people outside, looking up at the rubble, talking excitedly.

'It's been hit!' Remy said, horrified. What had happened to Methuselah? To Lisette and Noisette? Had they been up on that floor? Were they safe?

'It looks that way,' said Sheba. 'Although it's the only building around here that has been damaged. Seems a bit suspicious, don't you think?'

'I was just about to deduce that myself,' said Pyewacket.

'Perhaps we should leave,' said Sister Moon. She scanned the faces of the nearby crowd, looking for any of the Spider's thugs.

'Psssst!' A sound cut through the night, making them all glance up at the windows across the street. It came again, and Remy spotted its source: there, clinging to the side of a five-storey house like an insect, was a figure – long and thin as a beanpole, with silver hooks on his toes and fingers.

'It's Verlaine!' he said, pointing. The boy waved to them, and then scuttled round the edge of the building, disappearing into an alleyway.

'Let's follow him!' And Remy was off before anyone could stop him. The others ran after, ducking into the alleyway, half expecting there to be some kind of trap waiting for them. Luckily, the narrow passage was empty, apart from some piles of dirty sacking, and the elastic shape of Verlaine, unfolding himself from the building wall.

'Don't run off like that again!' Sister Moon scolded, catching up with Remy and grabbing him by the arm. She obviously wasn't used to this new, braver version of her son. One who had grown accustomed to the freedom of streets and crowds and cities.

'It's just Verlaine,' he explained. 'He's from the Théâtre. Don't you know him?'

Verlaine gave a bendy bow to them all. 'I'm afraid I joined after Sister Moon had left. I'm very glad to see you have rescued her.'

'What happened to the building?' Sheba asked. 'Was anybody hurt?'

'Thankfully not,' said Verlaine. 'But we have had to leave. Methuselah sent me to watch for you, and to bring you to him if you appeared. Can you climb?'

'Did Oliver Twist like porridge?' Pyewacket said, with a grin. Verlaine looked at him blankly. 'That means *yes*. Yes, we can climb.'

As if to prove it, Inji sprang to the wall, talons bared. Finding tiny claw-holds among the bricks, she scampered up the side and disappeared on to the roof.

'Actually, I might be a bit rusty,' said Pyewacket. He cracked his oversized knuckles and then felt about on the wall for a bit. Once he had a grip, he began to go up, hand over hand, building a rhythm as he went.

'Just a moment,' Sheba said. She bent to flick a switch on her leather ankle boots, and a set of spikes clicked out from the soles. She kicked them into the base of the wall, then clambered up it, digging her sharp fingernails into the cracks and crumbly mortar.

'I can't do any of that,' said Remy, watching the others make their way towards the roof.

'Don't worry,' said Sister Moon. 'You have many other talents, my darling.'

She bent so that he could clamber on to her back and then leapt at the wall, kicking off to send herself flying to the other side of the alley. She sprang from that wall too, then back and forth, back and forth, higher and higher with each jump, until she landed like a cat on the rooftop, even before Pyewacket and Sheba.

Verlaine joined them a few seconds later, and they took a moment to gaze across the rooftops of Paris. From the hill of Montmartre, they could see stacks of chimneys and points of steeples, lit up in jittering silhouettes by the cannon fire in the distance. Thousands of lights glittered in windows, like a blanket of stars. It was beautiful, Remy thought, wondering what all those long-dead skulls in the catacombs would have made of it. Was it anything like the Paris they had known? And what would it be like in another hundred years when he was just a pile of bones?

'Methuselah is in the churchyard, at the top of the hill,' said Verlaine. 'This way.'

He began to run along the rooftops, leaping and sliding down slopes of slate, dodging chimneys and clambering over balconies. The houses were all built together in long strips of unbroken roof. It was only once or twice that they had to leap over gaps or alleys to keep moving. From his mother's back, Remy looked down on the tiny figures in the streets below. Up here, he could properly feel the autumn wind, fresh on his face. Up here, he was safe from the Spider and her henchmen as they prowled somewhere far beneath him, in that crowded world of cobblestones, horse dung and carriages.

But, almost as soon as the rooftop sprint had begun, they were jumping down, from building to building, until they skipped along the ridgepole of a low shed and hopped to the ground.

They found themselves beside a high stone wall, covered with curtains of thick ivy. It stretched on down the narrow road, enclosing the churchyard, Remy presumed. He was looking for a gate or archway to get in when two shadows detached themselves from the wall and began to walk over. Between them, they carried a small wooden travelling chest.

'Zara!' the old man's cracked voice drifted out of the darkness. 'They found you! I'm so glad!'

'Hello, Methuselah,' Sister Moon said. She dipped her head to the other cloaked figure. 'Lisette. Noisette.'

Setting down the trunk, the grey-haired lady gave a shy wave. Another, child-sized hand pulled back the folds of the cloak and, for an instant, a tiny face could be seen there; all wide eyes, but smiling.

'I'm sorry your theatre got blown up,' said Remy.

'Ah, Remiel.' Methuselah doffed an imaginary

cap to him. 'You are safe. Don't worry about the Théâtre. It is just bricks and mortar, after all. And I have enough in the coffers to repair the damage, once this pesky war blows over. But I am afraid most of your travelling chests were destroyed in the blast. We were only able to save this small one.'

'Thank you,' said Sheba, bending to lift the trunk. 'This was the most important, anyway. The others just held clothes and snacks for Pyewacket.'

'The snacks were important to *me*,' Pyewacket muttered.

'Was it the cannons that did it?' Inji asked. 'Sheba seems to think otherwise.'

Methuselah gave them a serious look. 'It was indeed no cannon,' he said. 'That is why I had Verlaine bring you here via the rooftops. Three ruffians broke in through the front door. We saw them coming and guessed their intentions were evil, so we used one of our secret passages to hide. They were obviously searching for you. The blackguards must have blown up your chambers and luggage in frustration when they couldn't find you.'

'Three,' said Remy. 'D'Aramon must have got Toby Tall arrested, like he promised.'

'One less threat to worry about,' said Sheba. 'But that still leaves four of them, including the Spider.'

'We want to leave the city,' Inji said to Methuselah. 'Do you know a way out? Is it easy to escape?'

Methuselah shook his head, making his beard waggle like a winding snake. 'I have heard it has become most difficult. The ditch outside the city walls has been flooded, and there are many trenches and barricades in the fields beyond. Then, once you leave the safety of the surrounding French forts, there are the Prussian lines to cross. There is talk of snipers in every treetop and landmines along the roads.'

'Landmines?' Pyewacket asked. 'What are they?'

'A new invention,' Sheba explained. 'A stash of gunpowder or an explosive shell, buried under the ground. When you step on it, you ignite a fuse and then . . .'

'Kaboom,' Remy finished. It didn't sound like his daydream of a thrilling adventure: creeping between the enemy troops in the dark. In fact, it sounded like there would be a lot less creeping and much more exploding into tiny particles.

'Well,' Methuselah said. 'My troupe and I are going to find a secure place and lie low until it is safe for us to return home. You are all welcome to join us, if you wish.'

Remy looked up at his mother. Would she be able to put her tragic past behind her and stay with these old friends? Or was she still determined to keep them both shut off from the world and the pain it might cause?

In the end, Sheba answered for her.

'Thank you for the offer. And for everything you have done for us, but we really must leave Paris – as soon as possible. And we wouldn't want to put you in any more danger. We feel terrible that your theatre was damaged because of us.'

Methuselah took one of her hands and patted it. 'Don't worry, my dear. I have faced much worse before. Plagues, wars, erupting volcanoes ... I even lost a lovely house in the Great Fire that ate your very own London. We will be fine. We wish you luck, and if ever you are in the city again, you are always welcome to stay with us. Please give my regards to Marie when you see her.'

With that, the remaining members of the

Théâtre de Rêves turned and melted back into the shadows, leaving the Carnival standing alone on the street.

*

The night was drawing on by the time they made it back to Sister Moon's secret attic apartment. It had been a long, silent walk home, ducking into shady doorways whenever anyone walked past, watching every shadow and constantly listening for the ticking of sinister clockwork. Remy's mind was running with worries, fears and hopes about what might happen to him and his new group of friends. If they had to stay in Paris, could they avoid the Spider and her gang? If they did manage to find a way out, could he persuade his mother to stay with the Carnival? What would happen if the French army lost and the Prussians stormed the city?

The tangle of problems seemed endless. All he'd had to worry about a few days ago was finding his mother. What might happen next hadn't even occurred to him.

As soon as the door was bolted, Sheba set about

opening her trunk. It was filled with a range of bottles and trinkets that looked harmless, but Remy knew they would be lethal weapons of various kinds. He watched her take everything out and arrange it neatly on the kitchen table, next to the leather-bound notebook that held Spindlecrank's designs. The last thing she removed were the twin Bowie knives Remy had watched her pack, back in her London workshop.

'These are for you,' she said to Sister Moon, holding them out, hilt-first. 'I had them made quite a few years ago, when I thought there was a chance you might return to us.'

Moon took the knives by the handles. She stared at them, silent, for a long time, tilting them gently this way and that, watching as the gaslight sparked on the intricate ripples in the blades. Then she spun them both, one in each hand, round and round in a blur of silver. There was a thin whistle of air, and then they were sliding into the empty sheaths on her belt ... *thunk, thunk*!

'Thank you.' She bowed her head to Sheba, and then looked long and hard at Remy. 'I've been thinking,' she said. 'It was wrong of me to keep my boy shut away all his life. Wrong of me to shut myself away. I was trying to keep him safe, but in the end, I couldn't do that. Not on my own.'

'You did your best ...' Remy started to say, but she silenced him with a gentle hand on his head.

'Many times, I thought about running back to London,' she continued. 'But every time something stopped me. I suppose it was shame – that I couldn't save Azad. Or that I had brought my baby out in front of those people and allowed him to be put in danger. Some part of me even thought that I deserved to be on my own for what happened. That it was some kind of punishment.

'But I should have known that I was never on my own. Not really. I had a family all the time ... my Carnival family. The ones who risked their lives coming to help me, even though they hadn't seen me for nearly fifteen years. I don't think there could be anywhere safer for Remy and me, other than by your side.'

'What are you saying, Mother?' Remy felt a bubble of hope build up inside him. He prayed his mother's next words wouldn't pop it.

'I'm saying that – if they will allow us – we should

join forces with Sheba, Pyewacket and Inji from now on. That we shouldn't be on our own any more.'

'Mother!' Remy threw his arms around her, squeezing her tight.

'But,' she continued. 'There is one condition.'

'No, you can't use my indoor toilet,' said Pyewacket. 'Chamber pots and the outdoor privy for you, and think yourself lucky.'

'Not that,' said Sister Moon. 'It's leaving Paris. If it's as dangerous as Methuselah says – and he is always right about these things – then we should find another way to escape the city. I am not taking my child out on to a battlefield to be shot by a sniper or blown up by some bomb.'

Sheba left her unpacking and walked over to wrap her arms around Sister Moon. They held each other for a long time, while Pyewacket and Inji looked on, smiling.

'We're the Carnival of the Lost,' Sheba said, finally. 'If there *is* another way out of Paris, we will find it. Together, we can do anything.'

CHAPTER SIXTEEN

*In which Remy comes up
with a cunning plan.*

The next few weeks were difficult ones, as they spent their time racking their brains for a way to leave the city. Every night was broken by the thunder of Prussian cannons. Every day there were tales of buildings shattered by explosive shells.

In the streets, the mood had begun to change. The festival atmosphere that had made it seem more of a party than a war had vanished. There was no sign of the great French army coming to their rescue. A battle was fought in Châtillon, where the National Guard stormed out and tried to break through the

Prussian lines, but were forced to retreat in chaos. It had become clear to every Parisian that they were trapped and that they might very well lose the war, after all.

To make things worse, food was becoming scarce. All the flocks of sheep and cows had quickly been eaten. One day, when Sheba returned from a supply-buying expedition, she reported that she had seen a butcher selling horse meat. A week later, the same butcher was advertising dog and cat.[x]

'Make a joke about it and die,' Inji said to Pyewacket, whose mouth had been open, a smirk beginning on his face.

'Me? Joke about eating pussycats?' He pretended to look offended. 'I would never stoop so low. Now dogs, on the other hand ...'

'I'd be very careful about that too,' said Sheba, the hint of a growl in her voice.

'They'll be scoffing the animals in the zoo next,' Sister Moon said, shaking her head.

'Or rats,' said Sheba. 'There's plenty of them in Paris. They all seem to be coming out of the sewers, looking for food themselves.'[xi]

'Let's hope Marie doesn't find out,' said

Pyewacket. 'She'll be leading her own army in here to rescue the disgusting little blighters.'

The inside of Sister Moon's attic apartment had been turned into an operational headquarters. Sheets of paper and charcoal drawings covered the walls and floor. All sorts of plans for sneaking out of the city had been considered: trying to find a way through the catacombs (although nobody was very keen on going down there again); dressing in Prussian uniforms and marching through the barricades (except how were they going to get the uniforms? Or learn to speak German?); catapulting themselves over the wall (but what if they landed on an exploding mine?). Even disguising themselves as a small flock of sheep and munching their way out through the fields (which had been Pyewacket's only contribution).

It was proving impossible to discover a safe escape. And there was no sign of the siege ending before January, at the very least.

'I never thought I'd have to spend Christmas in a freezing-cold attic, eating fried rat instead of roasted goose,' said Pyewacket. 'It's just like when we were living with Plumpscuttle all over again.'

Among the plans and schemes sat Spindlecrank's notebook, next to Sheba's open chest full of gadgets. Remy had taken to flicking through its pages, wondering at the brilliant mind that had created such intricate, impossible designs and what had happened to the poor woman to turn her into the broken, stammering thing they had rescued.

The start of the book held precise, detailed drawings, labelled in beautiful copperplate handwriting. Towards the end, the pictures were pretty much just scribbles. More than once, Remy read the words 'must escape, must get free' in among the scrawling. *Well*, he supposed, *we did free her in the end. Maybe she will recover now she is out of that cage.*

'I was wondering,' he said to Sheba one day, as she tinkered with a spool of wire. 'The arms and legs Spindlecrank built for the Spider's gang . . . what are the tubes on them for?'

'From her designs, I would say they are pneumatic piping.' Sheba spoke with a small screwdriver gripped between her teeth. 'Compressed air operates pistons, allowing them to move like real limbs would.'

'And what are the tubes made out of?' he asked.

'India rubber, probably,' said Sheba. 'So they can bend and move without breaking.'

'Hmm,' said Remy, absent-mindedly tucking his hair behind his pointed ears.

'Why, have you thought of a way to disable them?' Sheba put down her wire device and stared at him with those gleaming eyes. Remy couldn't help but feel a little nervous under her intense gaze.

'Maybe,' he said. 'It's just that . . . the rest of the parts are all metal. So they would be hard to damage. But if you could burn or melt the rubber, then the limbs wouldn't work . . .'

To his surprise, Sheba threw back her head and whooped. 'That's brilliant! Of course!' She jumped up and began to rummage in her chest. 'I have some hydrochloric acid here somewhere. If we put it in a perfume-misting bottle, the spray might be enough. You'd have to be quite close, but it's a brilliant idea! Well done, Remy!'

From across the room, Remy noticed his mother staring at him and beaming. He pretended he hadn't seen, of course, but the toasty feeling of pride that began to glow in his chest made him smile too.

If it wasn't for the dwindling food supplies and the noisy cannons reminding him they were surrounded by an enemy army, Remy might even have enjoyed the time they spent cooped up together. But unfortunately their safety wasn't meant to last. One day, nearly four weeks into their stay, his mother rushed back into the apartment, slamming the door behind her.

'There's one outside,' she said, panting for breath. 'I don't think he saw me, but they must be on our trail.'

Remy went to the attic window and peered down at the street below. It was early evening and the gaslights were being lit. On the corner of the boulevard, standing among the straggles of Parisians heading home to wait out the latest bombardment, was Pierre. His narrow face was turning left and right, slowly scanning the doors and windows around him, looking for signs of his prey. From the sleeve of his greatcoat, the triple barrel of his gun-arm hung down, almost scraping the cobblestones.

His predator's gaze moved up and up, storey by

storey ... Remy ducked out of sight, well before he could be spotted.

'It's Pierre,' he said. 'The one with the rifle.'

'We shall have to move,' said Sheba, her face grim. 'Is there somewhere else we can stay?'

Sister Moon nodded. 'I know of a place,' she said. 'But it's less than ideal. Especially as the weather is getting colder. It's in Entrepôt, the tenth arrondissement.'

'It will have to do,' said Sheba. 'We can't risk staying here.'

And so they found themselves, in the early hours of the morning, travelling across the rooftops again. This time, they carried as many blankets as their arms would hold, with all of their remaining provisions tied inside. Stale baguettes of bread, scraps of dried sausage and the last few handfuls of coffee beans.

Sister Moon led them, under a sky that rocked and rumbled with distant explosions, to a shack built on a rooftop in the Rue de Dunkerque. Leant up against a teetering chimney stack, it appeared to have been made for keeping pigeons in. There were shelves of empty roosting boxes, covered in thick layers of droppings, and the place stank of rotten straw and birds. The walls were thin pieces of wood, riddled with holes. They let in streams of frosty draughts from all over, and the Carnival had to huddle together under layers of blankets to keep warm.

'We c-can't stay here,' Pyewacket stammered, through chattering teeth. Dawn seemed a long way off, but they were all shivering too much to fall asleep.

'M-maybe we won't have to,' said Remy. He was wrapped up in his mother's lap, but had managed to get an eye to a peephole in the shed wall. 'Look outside, everyone.'

With many moans about too much blanket being tugged this way or that, they all turned around and stared as Remy opened up the rickety window hatch, revealing a view of the rooftops loomed over by the arched windows and jutting statues of the Gare du Nord. There, floating above the station, was a ball of glowing light. Larger even than the shed they crouched in, it drifted upwards, carried out towards the city walls by the wind. Beneath it dangled a shallow basket, with the silhouettes of two figures sitting in it.

'That's it,' Remy said. 'Our way out of Paris!'

'A balloon!' His mother shook her head in disbelief, but she was laughing at the same time.

'It's perfect,' said Inji. 'Another genius idea, Remy.'

Pyewacket was less pleased. 'I am *not* going up in one of those things,' he said, wrapping himself in blankets again and sitting back down in a huff.

'Oh yes, you are,' said Sheba. She patted Remy on the back. 'Just as soon as we sneak into the station and steal one.'

*

Early the next morning, if you had been looking carefully, you would have seen three tiny figures, walking across the broad, sloping roof of the Gare du Nord. Two large, one small, they tiptoed along one of the steel girder struts, and then stopped when they got to the glass panes that ran the length of the rooftop, letting sunshine stream through to the station below. Carefully, making sure they didn't put any weight on the glass itself, they lay down on the roof and peered through the skylights.

It was Sheba, Sister Moon and Remy, his face and hands covered by his mask and gloves.

'Look,' said Sheba. 'They've turned the place into a balloon factory!'

The platforms, now empty of passengers, were filled instead by brightly coloured bags of varnished cotton, swathed in nets of rope. The tracks were full of workers, stitching fabric, wrapping rigging around baskets and tending the pipes that were pumping coal gas into the balloons, slowly inflating them. At one end of the station – their boiler fires gone cold – unused, silent steam engines looked on.

'Those ones near the end look ready,' said Remy. He pointed to where two balloons were tethered, just inside the open archways where the trains once ran out. Baskets hung below the floating spheres of their envelopes. Ropes trailed from these, down to the station platform, along with sandbags and two large ship's anchors.

'If we can pull them out on to the track, we can take off,' said Sister Moon.

'Do you think they will just let us have one?' Remy asked.

Sheba shook her head. 'I'm afraid that isn't very

likely,' she said. 'I spent this morning investigating the balloon service. They are using them to send letters and news out of Paris, for which there is a great demand. They aren't allowing passengers, or members of the public. And they have several guardsmen to protect them.'

Sister Moon sighed. Nothing ever seemed to be easy. 'When are they launching them?'

'At night only,' said Sheba. 'They are worried about Prussian sharpshooters bringing them down.'

'If we could distract everyone, maybe we could dash in and jump inside one,' Remy suggested.

Sheba nodded. 'A good old-fashioned diversion,' she said. 'And I have just the idea for it. Although Pyewacket isn't going to like it.'

'He never does,' said Sister Moon. She and Sheba shared a look, then laughed. Remy found himself wondering at his mother's secret life. At the adventures she and the Carnival must have had before she even met his father. It was funny how you thought you knew someone so completely, and yet they had been an entirely different person in another place, another time.

The three of them carefully stood and edged

down the sloping roof to the grappling rope they had used to clamber up the wall at the side of the station.

As they climbed back down to street level, clambering hand over hand, Remy looked up and – just for an instant – imagined he saw a figure standing on a rooftop in the Rue de Maubeuge, across the street.

But when he looked again, it had gone.

*

'I don't believe this,' Pyewacket said. He was wearing his night-vision goggles again – his round yellow eyes swimming behind the lenses – and standing in a low, brick tunnel, ankle-deep in stinking water. Remy was with him, unmasked now, as night had fallen. Up above them were the streets surrounding the Gare du Nord, the sound of horses' hooves and shouting voices filtering down through the stone and earth.

'Or rather, I *do* believe it,' Pyewacket continued. 'It's always me that gets the disgusting jobs: "Pyewacket, just go and stand in the poo-filled mud and wait for a monster to grab you." "Pyewacket, let some horrible villains capture you and then lay a trail with stink bombs." "Pyewacket, take these food scraps and go into the sewers so you can get eaten alive by starving rats." Why isn't Sheba ever used as bait? Why isn't she wading through stinking sludge in the dark?'

'I'm here too,' Remy said. He was holding a sack, half stuffed with leftover sausage and bread crusts. They had been dragging it along behind them, laying a scent trail of food that had already attracted a sizeable swarm of rats. He could hear them, scritching and scratching, just out of range of Pyewacket's red-tinted lantern. He could see the gleam of light reflected in hundreds of beady eyes.

'Yes, my boy, and you know how much I appreciate it.' Pyewacket slapped him on the back, nearly knocking him face first into the river of sewage. 'I shall make you my detective's assistant. All the best sleuths have one, you know. We shall be famous, you and I. Just think of all the crimes we will solve, all the stories that will be told about me – I mean, *us* . . .'

'Don't you think we've gathered enough rats now?' Remy interrupted. The odd one or two were beginning to become brave, dashing out of the shadows towards the sack, getting nearer and nearer each time before running back to their comrades. He had visions of them all suddenly rushing forward together, pouring over Pyewacket and himself, as well as the sack – gnawing them all to pieces with their sharp yellow teeth. When he had volunteered to help with the diversion, he had had no idea how terrifying a swarm of sewer rats could be.

'Yes, you're probably right,' said Pyewacket. He lifted Remy up, to where a ladder of iron rungs had been set into the brickwork. It led upwards towards a manhole cover in the Place de Roubaix, right in front of the Gare du Nord. 'Up you go, chuckaboo. Let's see if these rodents follow us like they did the Pied Piper.'

Remy began to clamber, his boots clanking against the metal rungs. He could hear Pyewacket huffing and puffing behind him, and beyond that, the skittering of tiny claws against the bricks. Thousands and thousands of them.

Sheba's plan had sounded simple. The tunnels and sewers of Paris were stuffed full of starving rats, ones that would go mad for the slightest scrap of food. If they could attract a swarm of them into the station, the guards and workers in the balloon factory would either run off in horror, or chase them for dinner. The rodents weren't the only ones in the city who were ready to eat just about anything.

And while their attention was taken away from those two launch-ready balloons, the remaining Carnival members would slip in, drag one out and then sail off into the night sky.

It had *sounded* simple, Remy realised, but the reality was proving a lot more dangerous. And a lot more stinky.

Finally making the top of the ladder, Remy stretched up to the manhole cover with one hand. But it was cast iron, and heavier than he was. He pushed against it as hard as he could – the thing didn't even budge. For one horrifying second, he thought they would be trapped in the tunnel, looking down as the tidal wave of rats crept up towards them . . . but then Pyewacket reached past him with one of those long, wiry arms and shoved the cover aside.

Clang! The night sky was revealed, along with a rush of cool, fresh air.

Remy drank in a lungful, and then hopped out, making sure to leave the sack dangling behind him. The rats *had* to follow them out of the sewer, or their disgusting trip through the city's bowels would have been for nothing.

'You know,' said Pyewacket, climbing out after him, 'I'm amazed your mother let you do this on your own. She's ever so protective of you, isn't she?'

Remy had been amazed as well. Although perhaps she thought it was safer. There were armed guardsmen inside the station, watching over the balloons. The other team ran the risk of getting spotted and shot.

'I suppose she didn't realise quite how many rats we were going to attract,' he said. He peered down into the sewer, which was boiling over with greasy, furry bodies. Tails lashed everywhere, like a mound of seething worms. They swelled up towards the surface, clawing and scrambling over each other to get at the sack.

'Bring it up now,' said Pyewacket. 'Nice and slow.'

Remy pulled on the rope, dragging the sack out into the open. There were already three rats clinging to it, ripping at the hessian with curved, hungry teeth. Their brothers, sisters, cousins and friends began to follow. A spreading puddle of slick, stinking fur that rippled up from the sewers and on to the cobblestones.

'It's working!' Remy cried, feeling a sickly mixture of excitement and disgust. He kept pulling the sack towards him as more and more rats spilled out on to the surface. 'What do we do now?'

'Give it here!' Pyewacket grabbed his hand, snatched the rope from him and began to run towards the doors of the station. There was quite a crowd of people there, all clamouring to get letters they had written taken out of Paris on the next balloon. A squad of guardsmen in their blue and crimson uniforms were trying to keep them in order, pushing them back as they waved crumpled envelopes in the air.

One of the guards noticed Pyewacket and Remy sprinting towards them, followed by what looked like a flood of brown, furry water. 'Hey! *Que faites-vous?*' he shouted.

Among the crowd, heads began to turn, but Pyewacket was running too fast to stop. At the last moment, he threw the sack towards the group of people at the doorway and changed course, turning sharp left. Remy, still clutching his hand, was dragged along with him, his feet leaving the floor. Looking over his shoulder, Remy saw the sack burst open on the cobblestones and the sea of rats begin to froth all over it, chasing hunks of sausage and stale bread crusts, scampering in among the letter-holding Parisians.

The screams began instantly. Ladies snatched up their skirts as rats ran around their feet. Men hopped from one leg to the other, trying to keep their trousers free of hungry rodents. One of the guards unslung his *tabatière* rifle and began firing shots at the rats – which then led to more panic as people thought the Prussians were storming the city.

Finally, an especially hungry man realised there were around a thousand hairy little meals running around in the open, ripe for the plucking. He began grabbing rats by the tails to take home and cook, and was soon copied by several others.

All in all, there was a mixture of screaming, shooting, cheering and wailing that drew all the guardsmen and balloon-makers from the station, not to mention hundreds of other people from the streets and houses all around.

'Our work here is done,' said Pyewacket, a tusky grin splitting his face. Remy laughed as well, and then they ran round the side of the station, on their way to meet up with the others.

*

With Remy on his back, Pyewacket clambered over the wall on to the deserted tracks. The station stood on their left, its cavernous archways like open mouths – gaping and empty. In the silent darkness, Remy could see the two balloons, tethered just inside the building. Their gas burners gave off a dim glow that lit up the swollen envelopes above. Somewhere, just inside, should be his mother and the others, untying the first balloon and getting it ready for take-off.

I'm going up into the sky, he thought, swirling butterflies of nerves tickling his insides. *What if we can't fly the thing? What if we crash, or get shot down by the Prussians? What if we can't steer it and blow out over the Atlantic Ocean?*

Pyewacket must have been having the same

thoughts. 'Just remember this was all *your* idea,' he said, as he set Remy down on the track next to him. 'Floating our way out of Paris, indeed. If it wasn't for the thought of having to eat rats and elephants, I would stay here and leave you lot to it.'

'I'm sure we'll be fine,' said Remy, more to persuade himself than anything. With one final check in his pocket to make sure Pamplemousse was safe, he began to follow Pyewacket into the station.

*

It was odd, being inside the empty space. Just a few weeks ago, it had been packed with people and trains. Great clouds of steam whooshing everywhere, the clank and screech of working metal. It had been deafening. Now the place was still and dark.

At the far end, outside the platform doors, the rats were still causing a commotion. Remy could hear shouts, screams and the odd gunshot. But the diversion wouldn't last long – they had to launch a balloon and climb on board as quickly as possible.

'Mother!' he whispered into the darkness, as loudly as he dared. 'We did it! Are you there?'

A hand appeared from the shadows and touched his shoulder. Remy almost screamed, but looked up to see his mother's familiar face, her night-black eyes looking down at him.

'Well done,' she whispered. 'We're about to bring the balloon out, but be quiet . . . Sheba thinks she can smell something.'

Peering into the gloom with his sensitive vision, Remy could make out the shapes of Inji and Sheba, crouched by the lines that tethered the first floating balloon to the platform. Sheba's head was tilted up, moving back and forth as she sniffed the air.

'Smell what?' he was about to ask, when a sound like a thunderclap rang out, echoing around the cavernous station. Sparks flew and metal *zinged* as a gunshot ricocheted off the stone, just inches from Remy's head.

'Nobody move!' A figure stepped out from a doorway on the far platform. A man with a long coat and a slender gun barrel instead of an arm.

Pierre.

The Spider's gang had found them.

There were more footsteps as others appeared: Ruby and Bébé, he presumed. And a fourth figure was with them too. A woman. He saw the silhouette of a wide bunch of crinoline skirts, a narrow waist, a long neck within a high-collared shirt and tresses of hair piled up beneath a veiled bonnet … could this be the Spider herself?

'My, my. What have we here? A band of evil balloon thieves?' She spoke in a genteel English accent, every consonant pronounced to perfection, like a society-trained lady. Except there was the slight trace of a lisp on the final 's'. It wasn't the voice Remy had expected a master criminal to use.

Inji stood, claws sliding from her fingertips. Remy felt his mother's every muscle tense. One of her hands inched towards the hilt of a Bowie knife.

'I said *nobody move*.' Pierre walked towards them, rifle raised. Ruby moved forward as well, her dagger-fingers slowly grinding together. She stopped just a few feet away from Remy and gave him a cruel smile.

'You must be the Spider,' Sheba called out to the new woman. 'We've already dealt with two of your mechanical henchmen. If you don't let us leave, things will go very badly for you. You have no idea who we are or what we are capable of.'

'Oh, but I disagree!' The woman moved closer, Pierre right beside her. 'I know you all very well. My friends and I have been shadowing you ever since we let young Remy here escape our clutches. And besides that – you and I are old friends, Sheba. I'm quite offended that you don't recognise me.'

There was silence for a long moment. Remy could see the smouldering embers of Sheba's amber eyes as they stared at the Spider through the darkness. Was he imagining it, or had they suddenly grown brighter? The glare was accompanied by a gasp of horror, and at the same time he heard his mother choke back a cry.

'It *can't* be!' Sheba whispered, her voice hoarse with shock. 'It's not possible.'

'I must say,' the Spider continued, 'it's *so* nice to see you again, Sheba. Haven't you grown into a beautiful young woman?'

CHAPTER
SEVENTEEN

*In which the Carnival find
themselves in the Spider's web.*

'**M**rs Crowley?' Sheba's voice was barely
more than a croak, choked thick with an
animal growl.

'The very same,' said the Spider. 'I expect you
thought me dead. Well, I'm sorry to disappoint you.
As you can see, I have been very busy in the last
few years. Building a criminal empire; capturing
that Spindlecrank woman and making her create my
team – my Hand, as I call them; plotting the utter
destruction of you and everyone you hold dear ...
The time has simply flown past!'

'Who is she?' Remy whispered to his mother.

'An old enemy,' she hissed back. 'A kidnapper, a thief and a murderer. We foiled her plans to kill innocent children, back when Sheba and I first met. She wanted to use their brains to cure her illness.'

'Destroy us, eh?' said Pyewacket. He was trying to sound brave, Remy could tell, but there was a tell-tale quiver in his voice. 'That didn't work out so well for you last time, did it? I seem to remember your brother being thrown in jail and *you* being shoved inside a burning pit. By *me*, in case you didn't realise.'

'No, it wasn't a roaring success,' admitted Mrs Crowley. 'But practice makes perfect.' She took another step closer, and Remy could see that her face was covered by a veil. Dark purple lace, decorated with cobwebs of silver thread. The same colour as her dress and gloves. 'And now – if you please – you will give me the map you stole from the catacombs.'

'You can't have it.' The words came out of Remy's mouth before he realised he was saying them. All eyes turned to him. Everyone looked as surprised as he was at the outburst. Running away and hiding was normally all he was good at. But the danger they had been through to get that piece of paper. The suffering they had all endured because of this gang of thugs . . . it had stuffed him full of so much anger, some of it had just bubbled out.

'Pierre,' said Mrs Crowley. 'Take aim at this child's forehead. Right between his horrid red eyes. If I can't see the map in five seconds, splatter his brains all over the platform.'

'Give it to them, Remy,' said his mother, her voice quiet but deadly serious.

'Quickly, Remy,' said Sheba. 'She *will* kill you. It isn't a bluff.'

Remy looked at them both and saw they meant what they said. Behind the anger that blazed in their eyes, there was cold fear. They looked like people who had just been surprised by a particularly large rattlesnake.

'Four,' said Mrs Crowley. 'Three. Two . . .'

'It's here!' Remy pulled Pamplemousse out of his pocket and held him up, the map poking from his eye.

'Very good,' said Mrs Crowley. She began to walk towards Remy, one gloved hand extended to take her prize.

'What do you want it for?' Inji said. Remy could almost feel her fur bristling from where he stood.

'What do you think?' Mrs Crowley replied, pausing to look at her. 'I want to find the Queen's Necklace. I want to hold it in my hands. And then I shall break it up and sell the diamonds for millions upon millions. And I will use that money to build an army of mechanised warriors. You may have stolen Spindlecrank's notebook, but I still have her plans.

'I shall forge scores of servants like my team, here. And then I shall use them to scrub your kind from the face of the Earth. My Hand and I will track you down, one by one, and wipe you out. From France, Britain, Russia, Italy ... every country in the world.'

'You would really use your fortune to do something so evil?' Sheba asked. 'Why do you hate *us* so much? Look at yourself. Unless you've found a cure in the past twenty years, you must look as different to everyday folk as we do. Your new friends too. We all get the same stares, the same comments. They would put *all* of us in a show to stare and laugh at, if they could.'

'*I am nothing like you!*' Mrs Crowley screamed

the words and they echoed around the empty station. 'Do you have any idea how much I hate you and your kind? Because of *you*, my plans were ruined, my hope of a cure lost. Because of *you*, my brother was arrested and imprisoned. Because of *you*, I almost died. I had to roam the streets, burnt, penniless, homeless ... I had to deal with criminals, with villains of the lowest kind. I had to steal, blackmail, murder, spy and cheat my way to where I am now. And every day, every *second*, I have been thinking and planning how I will have my revenge on you and your stupid Carnival!'

'What about your hired thugs?' Inji said, staring daggers at Pierre and the others. 'Do they know they've signed up for mass murder? Are they happy to get so much blood on their hands?'

Mrs Crowley laughed. 'Of course! They would do anything for me. I raised them from the gutter. Bébé was a starving beggar, dragging her legless body around the streets of Whitechapel. Ruby and Pierre were dying of gangrene in a grimy French hospital, too poor for proper care. Thom was cast out after his accident, reduced to robbing people in the street and Toby had his arm ruined in a fight. By one of *your* kind, no less; a monster with shark's teeth in its mouth. I gave them back their lives – made them *better* than they were before!'

Remy looked around at the faces of Ruby, Pierre and Bébé. They hadn't flinched when Crowley mentioned all the killing she expected them to do. In fact, they were all sporting ghoulish smiles, as if it was something they would enjoy.

'Now,' Mrs Crowley said, pointing at Remy. 'Give me the map.'

She began to walk towards him again, purple skirts swishing, hand outstretched for the roll of paper jutting from Pamplemousse's eye. Remy watched her coming, thinking of the map, of the fortune it would bring. And all those who would die because of it. People like him. Sons and daughters, mothers and fathers. Each with a life, with people that loved them, would miss them, would cry for them.

And he knew there was no way he could let this woman, this monster, have that wealth and that power.

He felt Mrs Crowley's slender fingers close around Pamplemousse, the lace of her gloves scraping against his hand. She gripped the doll's head, pulled it free, but – at the last instant – Remy snatched the map from his old friend's eye socket. He pulled it out and, not knowing how else to destroy it, shoved it in his mouth and began to chew.

The parchment was dry and dusty; the ink, as it dissolved on his tongue, bitter and sharp. He looked up, runny black bubbles dribbling from his mouth, and saw Mrs Crowley staring at him, a look of dumbfounded horror on her face.

'Now you've gone and done it,' said Pyewacket.

'She was going to kill us anyway,' said Inji. Remy could see his friend tensing, getting ready to spring.

'What have you done?' Mrs Crowley screamed. She threw Pamplemousse to the floor, where he exploded in a tinkle of breaking shards. 'What have you done, you vile little brat?!'

Still raging, she threw back her veil, revealing black-rimmed eyes blazing with spite. There was something wrong about how she looked: the top half of her face had looser skin, crow's feet, wrinkles and was currently scrunched up in fury. But the bottom half was smooth and flawless. Porcelain-white with pursed blood-red lips like a china doll. Emotionless, calm, still.

It's not real, Remy realised. Everything from her cheekbones down was a mask. If you looked closely, you could see where it joined her flesh. And there was another line, running down the middle, from nose to chin, as if the thing had been built in two pieces.

As Remy stared at it, the hairline crack began to widen. The mask split open, folding away on each side to reveal a mass of turning cogs and gears. They quietly ticked and clicked as both sides of Crowley's face slid backwards and a squat tube emerged from where her mouth should be. It looked like the barrel of some kind of gun.

'The Spider's Kiss!' Remy said. That had to be it ... the secret weapon whose plans had been torn from Spindlecrank's book.

Mrs Crowley's eyes stared down at him. 'I see Spindlecrank talked before you set her free,' she hissed. The words came through the gun barrel, from her mouth that was hidden behind. The effect was more than a little disturbing. 'I'm amazed she still had a mind left, after the fifteen years of torture I put her through. Although that will be nothing compared to the pain I am going to inflict on *you*.'

'The Kiss ...' Sheba asked, curious to the end. 'What does it do?'

'It's a gun, of course.' Mrs Crowley moved her head, pointing the barrel at each of them in turn. 'A very special one. Although I only have two shots, I'm afraid. Two poisonous fangs. Can you guess where they come from, Sister Moon?'

Remy looked up to see the blood drain from his mother's face. 'No,' she whispered. 'You didn't ...'

Mrs Crowley laughed. 'Oh yes, I did. It was easy, once I found out where you were hiding. Easy to bribe those thugs to start a riot in the theatre. Easy to goad your husband into attacking. I knew what would happen to him if he did. And then I just had to pay off the prison guards so I could take a little *souvenir* from his body ...'

What is she talking about? Remy played her words through again in his mind. *Two fangs ... his father ... the Spider's Kiss.* And then it all fell into place. She had forced Spindlecrank to make a weapon that fired a very particular type of ammunition: the teeth she had taken from his father before he had been executed. And the whole thing: the mob in the theatre, the arrest, kidnapping him and his mother, the map . . . it was all some elaborate way to get her revenge on the Carnival, and anyone who had been born different like them as well.

He was too shocked to act, too shocked to do anything but stand and stare at this woman, this *monster* who had ruined his life, and who was threatening to kill him even now. The loss of his father, all those years trapped in that Montmartre apartment, being made to run across the country in terror . . . it was all because of *her*.

'. . . and wouldn't it be fitting,' Mrs Crowley was saying, the words seeming to melt and swim together in Remy's stunned brain. 'Wouldn't it be *just perfect*, if your beloved's fangs were used to kill his wife and child?'

This isn't happening, Remy thought. *This must be a dream. A nightmare.*

He was still thinking it as the Spider's Kiss fired. A crack, a puff of smoke, and a bone-white fragment came shooting from Mrs Crowley's mouth. It was moving so fast, Remy only saw it as a flash. Something pointed, curved. The last remaining piece of his father, streaking towards him to end his life.

Except that the fang never reached its target.

There was a blur of motion from behind him. A *clang* as his mother batted away the tooth with the blade of her knife. Then she began to scream, even as she began moving at lightning speed.

First, she put an arm across Remy's chest and pulled him behind her, just as Pierre began to raise his gun-arm and swing it in their direction. With her other hand – in one liquid motion – she drew her second Bowie knife and sent it flying, end over end, towards Pierre.

Before the man could shoot, the hardened blade sliced into his arm at the shoulder. It hit the mechanical device hidden beneath his coat, crunching into the cogs and levers that triggered the rifle. Instead of firing, the contraption made a strange *twanging* sound, and Pierre was left staring at it in dismay.

But Sister Moon wasn't finished. Still screaming in rage, she ran at Mrs Crowley, leaping into the air to launch a flying kick at her. Remy also heard a feral hissing sound, and a blur that might have been Inji flashed past him, claws bared, flinging herself at the two villains.

Remembering that Ruby dagger-fingers had been

nearby, Remy turned, just in time to see her raising her blade-bunched fist to spear him.

'Remy! Catch!' Sheba yelled out to him. Looking to his right, he saw her fling a bottle towards him, sending it looping up into the air, sparkling as it began to tumble towards the ground.

Her perfume-mister, Remy remembered. *With the acid!*

He reached up with both hands to grab it, fingers fumbling for the rubber ball that worked the spray. Ruby was bringing her arm down now, those five slicing edges swishing towards him. Hoping he could remember where the India-rubber tubing was, he squirted the mister as hard as he could, spraying acid all over the top of Ruby's arm.

Instantly, the stuff began to eat through her clothes, burning great holes in her jacket. A terrible, chemical smell began to pour out, along with the sound of hissing air. Ruby jumped back, out of range of the acid, and stared at her arm. The limb was frozen in mid-stab. She strained as she tried to move it, but absolutely nothing happened.

'My arm!' she shrieked. 'What did you d—'

Her sentence remained unfinished, as a large

sandbag swung through the air, clunking her on the side of the head. She toppled to the ground unconscious, and there was Pyewacket, standing over her with a big grin on his face.

'What are you waiting for?' he shouted at Remy. 'Let's get out of here!'

Looking behind him, Remy saw that Pyewacket had untethered the first balloon and shoved it, so it began to float towards the open archway of the station. He still held the mooring rope in one of his great, flapping hands, but the balloon was already pulling away, as if it was hungry for the freedom of the night sky beyond.

'The others ...' Remy began, but Pyewacket stepped towards him, scooping him up with his free arm. Remy barely had time to reach down and grab for the broken pieces of Pamplemousse before he was heaved up, like a sandbag himself. Pyewacket ran alongside the balloon's basket with him and then threw him up, into the wicker carriage. Remy landed with a thump, among coils of rope and sacks of mail. The wind was knocked out of him, but he managed to scramble up and peer over the side of the basket.

Down below, he could see Pyewacket, towing

the balloon along the track as fast as he could. 'All aboard!' he shouted, as the craft sailed the last few feet out towards the opening.

Inji and his mother were still battling with Pierre and Mrs Crowley. Remy saw Inji rake her claws across Crowley's mask, knocking her to the floor. She grabbed the knife that jutted from Pierre's shoulder and wrenched it free, while Sister Moon kicked the man in the stomach. With her other knife, she rounded on the collapsed form of Mrs Crowley, but Inji pulled her away.

'The balloon!' she shouted in her ear. 'It's leaving!'

'No!' Sister Moon yelled back. 'She must pay for what she did!'

'But Remy's on board already!' Inji heaved at her arm again. 'He's drifting away!'

At the mention of her son's name, Sister Moon finally came to her senses. She allowed Inji to move her, and soon the pair were running towards the balloon.

'Hurry up!' Remy shouted, as the basket scraped against the brick of the archway. Just a few more moments and it would be free.

Sister Moon and Inji sprinted along and easily vaulted up, kicking off the wall and into the basket. His mother gave him a quick hug as she landed, but Remy was still leaning out, looking for Sheba. He caught sight of a crouched, wolfish shape, snarling and lashing at a thing that was half woman, half metal spider. His friend was caught in a battle with Bébé, and she was going to get left behind.

'Sheba!' Remy shouted, with every scrap of air his lungs could summon.

The growling wolf looked up, eyes blazing, and saw the balloon disappearing out of the station. With a final snap at Bébé, it turned and ran, bounding on all fours, reaching the edge of the platform just in time. Then it leapt, sailing through the air, to grasp the edge of the basket with its paws.

Remy, along with Inji, reached over to pull it in. By the time the creature had toppled into the basket, it had mostly returned to human form again. A rumpled Sheba looked up at them, fur and whiskers still shrinking back into her skin.

'Where's Pyewacket?' she said, forming the words around a mouthful of fangs.

'Here I come!' A familiar voice echoed from outside of the balloon and, a few seconds later, Pyewacket clambered up the mooring rope and hopped into the basket. The balloon bobbed under the weight and popped free of the station arch. They were out in the open, drifting steadily along the track.

'Why aren't we going up?' Inji asked. Although they were moving forward, they weren't getting any higher.

'It's too heavy,' Sheba said, flexing her shoulder joints as they popped back into their human-shaped place. 'We need to throw out some mailbags.'

'Better hurry,' said Pyewacket. 'That Pierre chap is trying to shoot at us with his gun-arm.'

Remy looked down, seeing Pierre had ripped off his jacket and was trying to get the machinery of his rifle working again.

Quickly, Inji and Pyewacket heaved all the mailbags over the side, letting them crash to the tracks below.

The balloon instantly began to lift, drifting higher and higher into the sky, until the Gare du Nord and all the buildings around it looked like a painted map, laid out beneath them. As they soared upwards, cresting an invisible wave, the wind took them, blowing them north, away from Paris.

'We did it!' Pyewacket shouted. 'We've escaped and we're on our way back to lovely London!' Everyone cheered, slapping each other's shoulders and hugging their friends with joy.

All except Sister Moon. Remy's mother had collapsed next to him, curled up in a miserable ball. He was about to go to her, when he realised his left hand was hurting. Looking at it, he saw he was still clutching the broken pieces of Pamplemousse. He was holding them so tightly that blood had begun to trickle between his fingers. Inji spotted it as well. She crouched beside him, gently lifting his palms so she could check how badly he was hurt.

'Oh, Remy,' she said. 'Your poor doll! I'm afraid he's smashed to pieces.'

Remy could only nod, looking at the mess of chips and shards that had once been his best friend.

Inji took a kerchief from her jacket pocket and carefully placed all the bits of Pamplemousse on it. When she had gathered them together, she tied the bundle in a tight knot and set it to one side.

'Pyewacket,' she said. 'Give me your hankie. Remy's hands are cut.'

Even then, Sister Moon didn't look up.

'Here,' said Pyewacket, tugging the pocket square from his waistcoat. 'It's mostly clean.'

Inji bit the middle with her sharp, feline teeth, then tore it in half. She began to wrap the fabric around Remy's palm.

'Is he badly hurt?' Sheba asked.

'Just a few scratches,' said Inji. 'I'm sure he'll be fine.'

'I'm sorry about the map,' Remy said. 'I know how valuable the Queen's Necklace was. But I just couldn't let her have it.'

'Don't worry,' said Pyewacket. 'I'm sure you memorised where it was hidden, didn't you? *Didn't you?*'

Remy stared up at Pyewacket's horrified face. The ink from the chewed map was still spread around his mouth in a blotted black stain. Millions and millions of pounds reduced to a spatter of inky dribble.

He suddenly felt like bursting into tears. He might even have done so, but – still not speaking – Sister Moon reached out an arm and pulled him into a hug.

'Forget about the map.' When Sister Moon spoke, it was barely a whisper. 'We don't need any treasure. We're together now. That's all that matters.'

'We'll take care of each other,' said Inji. 'We won't let that horrible Spider-woman come anywhere near us. She's stuck in Paris with no diamonds and barely any of her gang left. We'll probably never see her again.'

'I wouldn't be too sure of that,' said Pyewacket. He pointed back down towards the station, to the broad flat roof of the building with the stream of train tracks running into it, like a monster eating spaghetti.

There, rising up towards them, was the ball of a cotton envelope; glowing orange like a giant Chinese lantern. It was the second balloon, with Mrs Crowley and her remaining thugs in it, and it was chasing them.

CHAPTER EIGHTEEN

*In which the Carnival discover ballooning
is not as much fun as it looks.*

'I don't believe it!' Pyewacket shouted. 'Are we never going to be free of those metallic monsters?'

'I think they're gaining on us,' said Inji. 'They're moving much faster than we are.'

'They will be lighter than us,' Remy said, thinking aloud. 'There can only be three of them: Mrs Crowley, Pierre and Bébé. Ruby was knocked out cold.'

'I know,' said Pyewacket. '*I* was the one who finished her off. Didn't anyone see my move with the sandbag?'

Inji ignored him. 'Can Pierre shoot us from there? Can he knock us out of the sky?'

'I don't think so,' said Sheba. 'Sister Moon did a good job of messing up his gun-arm.'

'But is there any way for us to shoot at *them*?' Pyewacket said. They all began to search the basket they were sitting in. It seemed to hold nothing but a long coil of rope and some sandbags.

'All we have is *this*,' said Sheba, once they had finished looking. She held up the tiny clockwork pistol she had shown to Spindlecrank. The one she had said brought her luck.

'Fat lot of use that is going to be,' said Pyewacket. 'They'd have to be right on top of us for you to get a shot.'

'That might happen soon enough.' Sheba pointed below, to where the second balloon was now closer than ever. In a few short minutes, it would be upon them. All they could do was sit back and wait.

Remy poked his head over the basket edge – as far as he dared – and looked at the ground below.

They had drifted all the way out of Paris, past the buildings, over the wall and ditch, through the ring of armed forts that protected it. Now they were sailing over fields and villages, tiny trees like clumps of green cotton scattered everywhere. And in between – spread out in a loose circle of tents and trenches and barricades – was the Prussian army.

Remy had been given a set of toy soldiers for his eighth birthday. Delicately painted lead figures, he had named each of them and marched them on daring campaigns all over the floor of their small apartment back in Montmartre. The men below looked just like them: tiny people in smart uniforms, rifles and bayonets on their backs, parading in lines and squares as they followed their orders.

Even though it was night, there were still squads of men manning the fortifications they had carved out of fields and farmland. Deep ditches had been dug for them to take cover in, woodland had been hacked down to make way for clusters of white tents, and banks of earth had been thrown up to protect row upon row of cannons, each one the size of a large carriage.

As their balloon silently drifted over, skimming through the clouds, the giant guns began to fire. The mouth of each flared orange, puffed out a burst of smoke and then – a split second later – the *boom* reached the ears of the Carnival, high above. Sparks flew as the shells arced up and over the distant walls of Paris, to crunch their way through rooftops before detonating in balls of fire.

'Those guns . . .' Sheba whispered, as if speaking loudly might attract their attention. 'They are more powerful than anything I've ever seen . . .'

'It won't be long before they've flattened the forts and, after that, the walls,' said Pyewacket. 'We're best off heading back to England, where it's nice and safe.'

Inji was clutching the edge of the basket so tightly that Remy could hear her claws popping through the straw. 'If that's the future of war,' she said, 'then we're not safe anywhere. Heaven help us all.'

'What . . . what will happen if they spot us up here?' Remy asked. 'Won't they think we are French soldiers?'

'By the Artful Dodger's dodgiest dodging, he's right!' Pyewacket shouted. 'If they look up and see us, we're mutton on toast! We'll be target practice for the whole Prussian army!'

'Quick,' said Sheba, standing up and fiddling with the dials and levers on the gas burner. 'Help me turn this off. We can't let them spot the light.'

'But won't we sink if it's not heating up the balloon?' Inji asked. Even in the darkness, Remy could see that her face had gone pale.

'We should be all right for a short time,' said Sheba. 'At least far enough to get past the enemy lines. Then we can light it again. Hopefully.'

She turned a knob and the hiss of gas stopped. The floating basket that held them suddenly became very dark and very silent.

Ghosts in the air, they drifted, holding their breath as they passed over a particularly large Prussian camp. They were so intent on looking below, praying that a sniper didn't see them, they forgot all about the other threat to their lives: the balloon carrying Mrs Crowley.

Bang! A gunshot rang out, and a bullet whistled past them, making Remy almost jump out of the basket in fright. He stared at the army camp, wondering where the shot had come from, how it had sounded so *close*, when another blast sounded. It was followed by a scream from right beside him, and Sheba crumpled to the floor.

'It's them!' Inji shouted. 'They're right upon us! And Pierre has got his rifle working again!'

Everyone dived for cover, and Remy swivelled, in time to see the second balloon rear up next to them. Their burner was still blazing, and the orange fire lit up the three figures standing below: Mrs Crowley, Bébé and – with his gun-arm pointing straight at them – Pierre.

'Sheba!' Remy shouted, dropping to her side. She was clutching her shoulder and snarling in pain.

'Just a flesh wound,' she growled. 'Here, take my pistol. Stop Pierre . . .'

She handed him the little gun, its walnut grip slick with her blood. Remy stared at it, wondering what to do. He had never even fired a popgun before.

'Give it to me,' said Inji. 'I know how to use it.'

Remy tossed it across the basket to her, just as another gunshot rang out. A hole was ripped in the wicker, right next to Pyewacket's head.

'Blinking jibber jobbers!' he cried.

Inji caught the pistol, cranked the clockwork handle and knelt up, holding the gun out over the basket's edge. At the same moment, the other balloon collided with theirs, the bulbous envelopes bouncing off each other. As Crowley's craft began to move away, its basket swung towards them like a pendulum, bringing Pierre and his rifle close enough to almost touch.

'Have some of *this*,' Inji hissed, firing the pistol right at his face. There was a *twang*, and he staggered back, a tiny dart poking from his left eyebrow. He stared up at it, puzzled, and then collapsed like a toppling tree trunk.

'We're drifting away!' Remy heard Mrs Crowley shout. 'Grapple them! Get me close enough to kill Sheba with the Kiss!'

Kneeling up to peer over the side, he saw Mrs Crowley, her face folding open to reveal that gun barrel again, loaded with his father's second fang. Bébé stood next to her, holding what looked like a giant fish hook, tied to the end of a rope. She began swinging it, getting ready to throw it across and hook their basket like a prize kipper. It whirled around her head, glinting in their burner's firelight.

Firelight! That was it!

Remy darted across the basket until he was next to his mother, who was busy tearing strips off her shirt to bind Sheba's arm.

'Mother!' He grabbed her face and turned it towards him. 'Do you think you can hit their gas burner with a knife? Do you think you can make it blaze?'

Sister Moon turned to look at Mrs Crowley's balloon, slowly drifting away from them. Her ebony eyes took in the distance, the wind speed, the size of the target, all in the space of a blink.

'Yes,' she said. 'Why?'

'Just do it!' Remy shouted. 'Before she throws that hook!'

It was the first time Remy had ever dared order his mother to do anything, he realised, but she knew better than to question him. Trusting his judgement completely, she hooked a knife from its sheath, twirled it once around her fingers, and then let it fly across the empty space between the aircraft.

With perfect aim, the blade sliced through the gas-release nozzle, sending a golden jet of fire blazing up into the other balloon's canopy. The whole envelope lit up like a miniature model of the sun, lifting it ten, twenty feet above them.

It also alerted every single Prussian gunner on the ground below. Shouts of alarm rang out in German, followed by a hail of gunfire. Hundreds of bullets whickered through Mrs Crowley's basket in a hailstorm of lead. And then one or more punctured the canister of coal gas that hung under the burner, and the whole balloon burst into flames.

There were cheers from the army below, as the cotton envelope burned to tatters and the flaming basket began its long, slow fall to the ground. Staring at the blazing mess, Remy caught a brief glance of three figures tumbling, firelight glinting on metal and – although he was never sure if he just imagined it – the pale, white face of Mrs Crowley, cruel eyes about that porcelain mouth, still staring at them with hatred even as she vanished.

Remy and the others watched the wreckage, knowing their balloon would be next if any of the soldiers spotted it in the dark. They clutched each other, muttering prayers, their eyes scrunched shut in terror.

But maybe I can help us, Remy thought. Hiding was his speciality, after all, although he had never attempted to hide something so big.

Using all his strength, all his Gift, he reached out to the night and called it in. The purple blush from the underside of the clouds, the spidery streaks of black shadow from the trees beneath. Even the cold, endless emptiness that yawned between the stars in the sky. He summoned every last strand of darkness from as far as he could reach and flung it around their balloon, wrapping it in shade, turning it into the very opposite of the glowing sphere the soldiers had just destroyed.

And he waited.

The straw basket creaked as it swung. The ropes rubbed gently against each other. The cold, autumn breeze blew past him, chilling the tips of his ears.

Nobody dared speak. Nobody dared move. They stayed, huddled in a ball, curled around each other, until their legs and arms went to sleep. Until their toes began to prickle with pins and needles.

'Do you think it's safe?' Pyewacket finally asked, in a whisper that was little more than a breath.

Slowly, softly, keeping himself shrouded in night, Remy moved to the edge of the basket and looked over.

There was nothing underneath them but fields and cows.

To the south, now out of sight, the Prussian bombardment started up again. Flashes of light lit up the trees as the soldiers went back to their task of endlessly hammering the city walls.

They had done it. They were past the enemy lines and out over the countryside, free of the siege, free of Paris and – most of all – free of Mrs Crowley and her hateful minions.

CHAPTER
NINETEEN

In which Remy hasn't heard the last of Mrs Crowley.

G ently swaying in the sky, the balloon drifted among the clouds.

The wicker basket rocked from side to side, as soothing as a baby's cradle.

All around Remy, his friends were fast asleep. Inji lay, her head on Pyewacket's shoulder, purring gently as she snored. Sheba, her shoulder tightly bandaged, rested her head against a sandbag, twitching while she dreamed, making the odd whimper.

His mother slept with her arm around Remy, his face almost buried in her silky black hair. Being with her again was like coming home, even though their old apartment in Montmartre was many miles away now. Perhaps even blown to rubble by those enormous Prussian guns.

Everything worked out in the end, he thought. A warm feeling of relief flooded through him, filling him up from the tips of his pointed ears to his toes.

And now they were on their way to a new life. A new adventure. Floating wherever the balloon might take them, with nothing to worry them. As free as the birds in the sky.

He was just wondering what country they might land in, when he felt the basket shudder. It tilted to one side a little, as if something heavy had pulled at it.

'Mother?' He gave Sister Moon a nudge, but she didn't stir. The balloon shook again, harder this time. 'Inji? Sheba?' Remy called out to them, but nobody woke. He was on his own with whatever was jogging their airship.

And then he saw it: a hand covered in purple lace, gripping the side of the basket. Mrs Crowley hadn't fallen. Somehow, she had caught hold of their anchor rope, or perhaps used her grappling hook. Now she was trying to clamber in to use her vile Spider's Kiss on them.

Remy moved more quickly than he ever had in his life. With speed that almost matched his mother's, he leapt to the side of the basket and used the only weapon he had. He sank his fangs into the flesh of Mrs Crowley's hand, as deep as they could go.

'AAAAAAOOOWWW! What did you pigging well go and do that for?'

Remy sat up in bed, the nightmare about Mrs Crowley bursting into fragments, just as her flaming balloon canopy had done. Standing next to him, clutching one of his enormous hands, was Pyewacket. There were tears of pain in his goggling yellow eyes.

'I was only trying to wake you up,' he wailed. 'Why'd you go and bite me?'

'I'm so sorry.' Remy clapped a hand over his own mouth, speaking from behind it. 'I was having a bad dream . . .'

Pyewacket looked at his hand. There were two tiny dents on the back of it. Remy's fangs hadn't even broken the skin. 'Don't worry,' he said. 'It was only a nip. Hopefully I won't turn into a vampire. Was it Mrs Crowley again?'

Remy nodded. Most nights he was back in the balloon, watching as that evil woman crept on board. Most nights he woke up screaming.

'Well, don't worry, it was only a dream,' said Pyewacket. 'That old trout and her clockwork mask are blown to bits in a French field somewhere. She won't bother you again. You're safe here with us. Come on, let's go downstairs and see if Father Christmas has been.'

Remy threw back the covers and climbed out of bed, pausing to pull on his dressing gown. The room he had been nursed in, that first day he had met the Carnival, was now his own bedroom. A wardrobe of clothes stood in the corner, and there was a desk beneath the window, covered in ink bottles and exercise books. Sheba had decided to give him an education: physics, algebra, Latin and especially chemistry. They were already working on a cream that might be able to block the harmful rays of the sun from his skin.

His mother had moved into her own chambers on the floor below, and she seemed happier and more relaxed than she had ever been. It had been over a month since they had returned from France and nobody had mentioned going back – Remy hoped and prayed that they wouldn't mention it. He knew they would have to return one day. They had a home there, after all. But the thought of leaving all his new friends and going back to that lonely apartment . . .

However, today was not the day to think about it.

Now that the horror of the dream had evaporated, Remy felt himself bubbling up with excitement. *Christmas morning!* And the first Christmas he had spent with anyone other than his mother.

He ran down the stairs, pausing only to peer out of a landing window. Fat, feathery flakes of snow were falling, and the street was already covered in a white blanket. Later, he might put on his mask and gloves and have a snowball fight with Pyewacket, Inji and Sil. But first: *presents.*

When he walked into the front parlour there was a cheer. Everyone was there, sitting around a crackling fire. Sheba was serving breakfast. Inji and Sil held hands on the sofa and Glyph sat cross-legged on the hearthrug, practising card tricks.

His mother appeared from behind the Christmas tree. She scooped him up and squeezed him tight.

'*Joyeux Noël,*' she said in his ear, before kissing him.

'Merry Christmas, Mother,' he replied. 'Merry Christmas, everyone.'

'Merry blooming Christmas!' Pyewacket shouted. 'Now where's those pressies?'

Stockings had been hung on the mantelpiece, and Sheba took them down and handed them out. There was much rustling and tearing of tissue paper as the presents were opened.

Pyewacket received a new magnifying glass, for his sleuthing. Glyph got a set of personalised playing cards; Sil a model horse and cart; Inji a new waistcoat and Sheba a beautiful leather-bound notebook with the creamiest paper pages (Remy had gone to the shop with Sister Moon to choose it especially).

Sister Moon had a replacement Bowie knife for the one she'd lost in the battle, and Remy had the biggest haul of all: a new – more comfortable – mask, a chemistry set, a silver case of business cards that read 'Remiel Moon – Detective's Apprentice', and some lead soldiers, just like the ones he had treasured back in Paris.

He looked at his spread of presents, feeling grateful tears filling up his eyes.

'There's something else in the bottom of your stocking,' Sheba said. 'Something special. From us all.'

With curious fingers, Remy reached in and drew out a small package, about the size of a tangerine. It was round and hard, with odd bumps here and there. A familiar shape that fitted into his hand like an old memory.

Could it be? Tearing off the paper, a lump already in his throat, he revealed a small, china doll's head. Nose worn smooth, paint rubbed away in patches and one wonky eye looking up at him . . . it was his old friend, his one and only gift from his father.

'Pamplemousse!' Remy held the little doll up and kissed it, running his fingers over the worn ears and chin. But something was different . . . there were lines of gleaming yellow sketched all over Pamplemousse's head. His broken pieces had been stitched together with seams of actual gold.

'It's a tradition from Japan that I heard about,' Sheba explained. 'When a precious bowl or ornament gets broken, they repair it with gold. It's to remember what happened, to celebrate it as part of what makes the item special. The accident that smashed it becomes a part of its beauty. It makes it stronger. Unique.'

'A bit like you and me,' said Sister Moon. 'All your life, I have been running away from what happened to us, trying to hide from it so nothing bad would hurt us again. But I should have faced up to it. I should have dealt with it and made it a part of me. I should have used it to be stronger. To live my life even though a terrible thing had happened. I realise that now. And I know that is what your father would have wanted.'

'You were only trying to keep us safe, Mother.' Remy put a hand against her cheek.

'But I stopped you from living,' she said. 'I kept you from these people, these friends you should have known.'

'This *family* you should have known,' Inji corrected. Beside her, Sil looked up from his toy cart to clap his hands.

'Does this mean ...' Remy whispered the words into Sister Moon's ear. 'Does this mean we can stay?'

'As long as we want,' Sister Moon replied. 'Or as long as the Carnival will have us.'

'This is your home,' said Sheba, beaming. 'It wouldn't be the Carnival without you.'

'We should really rename it "Carnival of the Found",' said Inji.

'I'll do the jokes, thank you very much,' said Pyewacket. 'In fact, I've been thinking about changing my career. What do you all reckon to me becoming a comedian?'

The groans could be heard all the way down Paradise Street, as could the cheers that came after, the singing and the feasting. The sounds rose up, mingling with the church bells that rang all over London, shouting out that the one thousand, eight hundred and seventieth Christmas was going to be the merriest of them all.

NOTES

i. The famous *Dracula* by Bram Stoker was not published until 1897, so the most well-known vampire at this time was Varney, the hero (or villain) of several Penny Dreadful novels that first appeared in 1845.

ii. It would have surprised most Victorians: women weren't expected to leave the house unless they were wearing at least seven layers of skirts, petticoats and corsets.

iii. A term that described someone dressed up in their best clothes. Although why you would put them on just for the afternoon is a mystery.

iv. Little did Mama Rat know that the second Empire was ending even as she spoke, and the third Republic beginning. Studying French history is only slightly less difficult than performing brain surgery.

v. Prussia was the name of the countries and states that would become Germany. It has absolutely nothing to do with Russia.

vi. France had been at war with Prussia since July. It all began – quite ridiculously – over a telegram that made the French Emperor, Louis Napoleon, very cross. Everyone in Europe expected the mighty France to win, but the Prussians had secretly been building up their army with modern cannons and guns, and had given the French army several good kickings.

vii. The river that runs through Paris. Your dad probably has a joke about falling off a boat and 'going in-Seine'.

viii. Paris expanded in 1860, swallowing up several of the small towns that surrounded it. It also got its nice new wall and defensive forts that were currently being tested by the Prussian army.

ix. A strange term, which meant 'messing about in the streets'. Although what kind of messing exactly isn't clear . . .

x. At first people were disgusted by butchers

selling dog and cat meat, but after starving for a while, they soon got used to it. One hungry citizen began to fatten his cat up for Christmas dinner, planning to serve it on a plate, surrounded by stuffed mice.

xi. They did, in fact, have to eat both rats *and* zoo animals. After Christmas, when food began to get really scarce, Castor and Pollux, the zoo's twin elephants, were shot for their meat. Although nobody was brave enough to try eating the lions and tigers.

Welcome to the magical World of Podkin One-Ear!

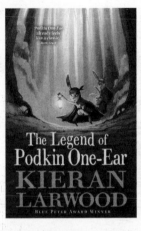

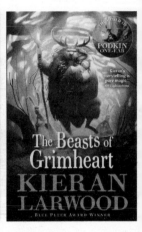

Winner – Blue Peter Book Award
Winner – Prix Sorcières